NOT PLAYING FAIR

TERRI OSBURN

DEDICATION

For my Favorite Boys. You were both a help and a hindrance for this one.

ALSO BY TERRI OSBURN

Find them all here

The NOT Series

Not You Again

Anchor Island Series

Meant To Be

Up To The Challenge

Home To Stay

More To Give

In Over Her Head

Christmas On Anchor Island*

*coming Oct 2021

Ardent Springs Series

His First And Last

Our Now And Forever

My One And Only

Her Hopes And Dreams

The Last In Love

Shooting Stars Series

Rising Star

Falling Star

Wishing On A Star

Among The Stars

Stand-Alones

Ask Me To Stay

Wrecked

Awakening Anna

CHAPTER ONE

MOMENTS LIKE THESE WERE THE REASON I LOVED my job.

"Ms. Megan, Jeremy has his feet on his chair, and the chairs don't like that."

As a librarian, my favorite patrons were our children's reading group, and I was fortunate to work with them several days a week. During our last story time, we read a book in which chairs aired their grievances over how they were treated. It was good to know that Lucy had been paying attention.

"Can you nicely remind him to put his feet back on the floor?" I asked.

"I can do that," she said, always ready to accept a mission.

Though some might say she spent too much time policing the other children, I saw Lucy as a future leader and wouldn't dare dim her light for anything. She simply needed to learn diplomacy, but she was only eight. There were people ten times her age who had yet to learn that particular skill.

"Did everyone find a book?" I asked. After I read to them, each child was encouraged to then choose a book to read on their own.

"Yes, Ms. Megan," echoed back to me from around the room.

The children's reading program was held in the downstairs meeting room of the library, which meant the patrons upstairs were not disturbed. Other branches in the system had special rooms just for the children's books, but we didn't have that kind of space. Moving to a larger building or adding on simply wasn't an option since we were housed in our original location built in the 1890s.

One of my favorite pictures in the library dated back to the 1910s. In it, women and children sat together at long tables in the center of the main library space. When you looked away from the picture you could see that very little had changed. Even the enormous light fixtures hanging from the twenty-foot-high ceiling were the same.

"Ms. Megan, will you read this to me?" said Ruby Laramie while tugging at the skirt of my dress.

We weren't supposed to have favorites among the children, but I couldn't help but love Ruby. She'd been coming to the reading program since she was five, which was two years ago now. Even then she'd been able to read well above her grade level, yet she often asked me to read to her despite her skills.

"This is your time to read by yourself," I said, seeing she'd picked one of her favorite books.

At the age of three, Ruby had been in a car accident that had taken her mother's life and left the child's face partially scarred from the fire that had nearly killed her as well. The book in her hands was called *Eyes That Kiss in the Corners* and was about a young girl learning to find the beauty in her Asian-shaped eyes. It wasn't hard to figure out why Ruby related to a story about accepting what made one special, even when that something also made her different.

"But I like when *you* read it," she said.

We'd had this discussion before. "If I read to you, then I have to read to everyone, and I already did that. Why don't you read it to me?"

Tucking the book against her chest, she dropped her eyes to the floor. "Then everyone will look at me."

"Why shouldn't they look at you?"

Her tiny shoulders shrugged as she said, "Never mind."

She ambled to a chair in the corner, and I spotted Elijah still searching the shelves. Like Ruby, he stood out from the other children, though his difference was easier to hide. Elijah had been born with only one ear so he kept his hair long to cover the bare space where an ear should be.

I tapped him on the shoulder. "Have you not found a book yet?"

"I don't know what to get."

"I happen to know that Ruby is looking for someone to read to. Why don't you ask her if you can listen?"

Bright-blue eyes found the little girl alone in the corner. "Do you think she'd let me?"

I nodded. "I'm sure she would."

Bottom lip slightly protruding, he debated for several seconds before nodding. "Okay, I'll ask her."

Resisting the urge to escort him over, I watched him approach her only to stand in silence for several seconds until Ruby noticed him. There was a brief exchange before Elijah pulled a chair over, placing it so that she would be on the side he could hear from, and then she turned back the pages to start reading from the beginning.

This was what made my job so rewarding. Not only introducing children to stories and helping them fall in love with the written word, but teaching them to share that love with those around them.

"I need to get back upstairs," I told Ms. Patty, a retired teacher who volunteered at the library and loved working with the children as much as I did. "If you need me, just call my desk."

"I've got this," she replied. "You go on."

I took one more walk around the room to make sure everyone was settled in before stepping out and heading upstairs. Before I could reach my desk, my coworker cut me off.

"I have a question for you," said Miriam Webster. Yes, that was the actual real name of my fellow librarian. A couple inches taller than I was and on the round side, Miriam wore cat-eye glasses, beautiful braids that danced around her head, and her favorite shade of Pixy Pink lipstick, which she never let fade from her lips. "What if we're all living in a simulation and none of this is real?"

She'd obviously listened to another conspiracy theory podcast on the way to work today. This happened several times a week and led to conversations on topics ranging from lizard people to political intrigue to aliens living among us. As the voice of reason in these discussions, I played my part.

"What if we are? Would knowing that change anything?"

As she often did when faced with a rational response, Miriam visibly deflated. "I guess not."

"Exactly." Pointing to the cart at the end of the front desk, I said, "These books still have to be reshelved, and no simulation is going to change that."

"You're no fun," she replied with a grin. This was a routine we'd performed countless times.

"Who is no fun?" asked Cassie O'Malley, a young woman who had become a regular visitor recently.

"Megan has no imagination," Miriam replied.

I rolled my eyes as Cassie caught on right away.

"Shot down another theory, didn't you? What was it this time?"

"That we're living in a simulation," I replied. I'd never set out to be a skeptic. I'd simply been born with a deep-seated practicality that prevented me from entertaining such far-flung ideas. "To be fair, I did not *shoot down* the theory. I simply pointed out that true or not, our lives will continue just as they are so there's no real point to the debate."

"But it's fun," Cassie replied with a shrug. "Nothing wrong with tossing around ideas for the fun of it."

I was not against doing things *for the fun of it*. My idea of fun simply differed from Miriam's. And most other people's, unfortunately.

"Okay then," I conceded, motioning with my hands to indicate the room around us. "What if this *is* all a simulation? What then?"

Miriam and Cassie exchanged a puzzled look. "I don't know," Miriam said, giving the library patron a pleading expression.

"Don't look at me," Cassie said. "It's your theory."

"It isn't *my* theory. I was just asking."

The two fell into silence and after several seconds, I said, "Well, that was fun. Cassie, how is your research going?"

The young woman had traveled from California to Pittsburgh to learn more about her family.

"Slow, but I've got a lead so I'm hopeful."

"Let us know if we can help."

"Ms. Knox, I need to see you."

I turned to find Jeffrey Chamberlain standing in the doorway to the stairs I'd just come up. He'd been my boss for a month now and had yet to use my first name. There were days I doubted he remembered it.

"Yes, sir."

As he disappeared from sight, Miriam mumbled, "Good luck."

"Does he ever actually come up here?" Cassie asked. Jeffrey's office was downstairs, across the hall from the meeting room. "I've never seen him *in* the library."

"Almost never," Miriam replied. "I think he spends the day playing games on his computer, but I can't prove it."

"Managing three branches is a lot of work," I said in his defense. Not that I didn't agree with my coworker's theory—for once—but library employees gossiping with a patron about their boss was not a good idea. "I'm sure once he gets settled in he'll be more accessible."

"Let's hope not," Miriam murmured. I shot her a warning glance and she changed her tune. "That's true that he has a lot on his plate. Nancy was wonderful, but not the most organized person. Taking over for her probably hasn't been easy."

Defending one boss by criticizing another wasn't exactly a step in the right direction. Nancy Kitchens had overseen three branches of the library system for twenty years. Upon her retirement over the summer, Jeffrey had been hired, and the atmosphere of the library had changed immediately. Where Nancy had created a sense of family among the staff, Jeffrey felt more like a warden. He never smiled on the rare occasions we did see him, and he'd made no effort to get to know us beyond our assigned duties.

The monthly potluck lunches were over. The group chat was gone. The Sunday check-ins and occasional after-work dinners were no more.

It was a testament to how much I loved my job *and* my coworkers that I hadn't yet asked for a transfer. With nineteen branches in the system, I certainly had that option, but this one was closest to my apartment, and I didn't only love what I did, I loved *where* I did it. I wouldn't let Jeffrey Chamberlain take that away from me.

"If you'll start reshelving these books, I'll take over when I come back," I said. "I'm sure whatever he wants won't take long." The few times I'd been summoned to his office, the questions had been simple and easy to answer. Where was this? What was the history of that? Nothing that required much of my time, thankfully.

"No worries," Miriam replied. "I've got this."

I crossed the short expanse back to the stairway, sliding a copy of *The McGraw-Hill Encyclopedia of Science and Technology* back into place on my way. These brief meetings were never enjoyable, but for some inexplicable reason, I found myself dreading this encounter more than usual. Dismissing the baseless apprehension, I descended the stairs and tapped on Jeffrey's half-open office door.

"What did you need?" I asked, hoping the question might be a quick one.

"Sit down, Ms. Knox," he said in his deep, raspy voice. So much for quick.

Though smoking was not permitted in the library, Jeffrey Chamberlain carried a heavy scent of cigar smoke that made the back of my throat itch. I could only assume the smell clung to his clothing, as he'd added few personal items to what used to be Nancy's cheery little office. The place could use a few of her plants to soak up the bitter tobacco smell.

As I settled into the navy-blue upholstered chair, I gripped the narrow wooden arms and told myself not to breathe too deeply.

"I wanted to let you know that changes are coming," he began.

My chest tightened. "Changes?"

"The head office has brought in a consultant to show us where we can make cuts." Looking at me for the first time since I'd walked in, he slid a sheet of paper my way. "The managers were asked to submit a list of programs conducted at each branch. I assume he'll start by looking at these."

I knew this list, of course. I'd had a hand in creating several of the programs. At the top was the children's reading program, which was the longest running program in the entire system. One that originated in this building more than a hundred years ago and was quite possibly the first of its kind in the entire country. I searched for some indication that the programs were weighted. An asterisk or other mark to indicate the ones that should be kept.

There was nothing.

"Surely you let them know that the children's program can't be cut."

"Everything is on the table," he replied. "I'll do my best to keep what we can, but there are no guarantees."

No guarantees my foot.

"That program cannot be *on the table*," I said, popping out of my chair. "Not only has it been an important part of this library for well over a century, but it's also a crucial source of learning and support for the children in this area. Especially those without the financial resources to get that support elsewhere."

Unmoved, Jeffrey slowly lifted his eyes to mine. "Ms. Knox, I am sharing this information as a courtesy so that you might be prepared should we need to eliminate these programs. As I said, I will do what I can, but you should be ready to make cuts when the time comes."

His choice of the word *when* instead of *if* made my teeth grind. The man felt no connection whatsoever to what we did here. He didn't care about the staff, and he clearly didn't care about the patrons we served. I wanted desperately to ask why he'd even taken this job, but as I preferred not to lose my own, I clamped my lips shut.

After a tense pause, he said, "If more information is requested about the programs, I'll let you know."

He'd have to, considering he hadn't taken the time to even ask about them before now. No doubt he'd take credit for whatever information I provided.

I would not let this go without a fight. "Will you at least make sure I get the opportunity to defend the program if necessary?"

Sighing as if exhausted by my persistence, he waved a hand in the air. "I'll see what I can do."

And I would do the same, even if it meant going over Jeffrey's head. The kids across the hall needed us. They needed one safe place where they could explore the world that lay ahead of them. Most were from broken homes and had already learned some harsh realities far beyond their years. Here, in our program, they could be innocent, curious, and supported.

Jeffrey Chamberlain may not be willing to fight for them, but I was.

CHAPTER TWO

At the end of the day, I was still fuming.

"Wow," Miriam said. "You only type that loudly when you're really mad."

I hadn't noticed the abuse I was giving the keyboard. Flexing my fingers, I said, "I'm forming a plan to deal with this consultant situation."

The logic of bringing in a random stranger to fix anything had never made sense to me. Yes, those who knew the programs well might be more attached to them, but that didn't mean that *we* weren't the best ones to determine what *could* and *could not* be cut.

"That's a good idea." Settling into her chair farther down the counter, she said, "You don't think they'll let some of *us* go, do you?"

I'd been so preoccupied with the programs that I hadn't even considered the idea of staff cuts.

"I don't know. Jeffrey didn't mention that."

Miriam returned to her feet to pace the small area between our workspaces. "I don't want to work anywhere else. What am I going to do?"

We already operated with a small staff so I couldn't see this being an issue. "I really don't think our jobs are at stake."

"Of course, *yours* isn't," she said, waving a finger in my direction. "You've been here for five years and you practically run the place."

She was going off the rails quickly. "Miriam, you've been here two years longer than I have. You trained me, remember?"

"That's right! I'm old. I'll be the first to go."

"You're thirty-five," I pointed out.

"That's old in librarian years."

If anything, librarian years worked the opposite way.

"Miriam, you are not old and there's no reason to panic. At least not about your job. Jeffrey says they're reviewing *the programs* for potential cuts. He never mentioned the staff."

Eyes wide, she sat again. "But all of our programs are important. We're the ones who are disposable."

Not technically true on the programs side. I could think of three off the top of my head that would not be missed, but getting rid of them would also not save the library a substantial amount of money. As for being disposable as employees, that was ridiculous. Yes, we could all be replaced, but where would be the savings if they let us go? They'd still have to pay the replacements.

"First off, *we* are not disposable, and Jeffrey gave me absolutely no reason to believe that we should fear for our jobs. So let's not borrow trouble that doesn't exist. Secondly, regardless of how important we think the programs are, the cuts are going to come and we need to be ready to protect the ones at the top of the list."

"The list?" she repeated.

"The one I'm making right now." I turned back to my computer. "I want to be prepared when the time comes."

I hadn't helped lead my high school debate team to three state championships without learning how to argue a case. If I'd been more outgoing, I might have pursued a law degree, but I preferred fiction to legal briefs, and the thought of standing at the front of a courtroom made me nauseated.

Miriam rolled her chair over beside mine. "What do you have so far?" I turned my monitor so she could see. "Children's reading, ESL, diverse history collection. What about the seniors program?"

Everything from computers and social media training to how to avoid the heartless scammers who preyed on the elderly were umbrellaed under one program.

"That should be next." I updated the list. "I'm not sure about the speakers program. It's one of the more expensive options so there would be significant savings if we let it go."

My coworker sighed. "I look forward to those though. And the speakers bring more people into the library."

"True, but I'd rather see that one go than the rest of these." My phone dinged with a reminder and I checked the screen. "Oh, crap," I said after reading the message. "I forgot about practice tonight."

"Is it softball season again?" Miriam asked.

"Yes, and it's a new team so I shouldn't be late. Practice starts at six and I still have to change clothes." I checked the time in the corner of my monitor. "That means I need to leave now."

"Oh, me, too." She pushed backward and rolled to her area. "Devon is taking me to dinner, and I want plenty of time to freshen up before he picks me up."

Miriam met Devon through a dating app several weeks ago, and though I had yet to be introduced, the stories I'd heard and the smile he put on her face were enough to make me like him already.

"This is getting serious?" I asked.

A blush covered her cheeks as her eyelashes fluttered. "I hope so. This is the one-month anniversary of our first date. I didn't even realize it until he brought it up."

I so hoped this worked out for her. A good man was hard to find. As I knew all too well.

"Where's he taking you?" I asked as I saved the file and shut down my computer.

Miriam giggled. "I have no idea. He said he wants to surprise me."

"Are you ladies headed out?" asked Thomas, a fellow librarian whose shift went through the evening.

"We are." I turned off my monitor before retrieving my purse from the bottom desk drawer. "Would you make sure that the last cart is emptied before close, and that the meeting room is set up for the writing group in the morning?"

"Will do," he said with a nod. "I hear you're on the same team as Fletcher this fall."

Thomas had introduced me to Fletcher Howard—the man I dated for three years before we broke up eight months ago. Well, we didn't break up so much as he dumped me. Like an idiot, I never saw it coming. Fletcher had used the insulting *it's not you, it's me* line, with the kicker of *we're just too different.*

By different, he'd meant that he was interesting and outgoing and fun and that I was not. He wasn't wrong. An introverted homebody whose idea of a good time was a quiet Saturday night with a good book didn't exactly scream life of the party.

Yet I'd attended countless parties to make him happy. That clearly had not been enough.

"Yes, I am. I don't know much about the rest of the team, but I'll meet them tonight."

"Wait," he said as I rose from my chair and tucked it up under the desk. "You do know that Fiona Lewis is on the team, too, right?"

The name meant nothing to me. "Fiona?"

"Fletcher's *new* girlfriend."

I wasn't aware that Fletcher *had* a new girlfriend. The announcement took the wind out of me. I'd had enough time since the breakup to convince myself that Fletcher had not been the love of my life, but that didn't mean I wanted to spend my fall watching him become the love of someone else's.

Going for indifference, I said, "No, I hadn't heard. So long as she can play ball, I see no problem."

The vise squeezing my lungs said differently.

"Oh, yeah. She played for Duquesne about five years ago," he said. "She's really good."

Jaw tight, I tugged my purse onto my shoulder. "Great. Then we should have a winning season."

I strolled around my coworker, keeping my chin up and a smile on my face. Miriam caught up to me at the top of the stairs.

"Are you okay?" she whispered.

"I'm fine," I said, much too cheerily. "Why wouldn't I be?"

"Megan, that piece of crap Fletcher broke your heart, and now he's bringing his new girlfriend into the thing you two shared the most. That's a big deal."

My skills on the ball field *had* been what drew Fletcher to ask me out in the first place. We were both competitive, and though these small-time games were only for fun and bragging rights, they were something we'd done together as a couple. And now he was a couple with someone else.

"I'm fine. Really. I always knew he'd move on." Fletcher wasn't the type to stay single for long. He fed on attention. If anything, I felt bad for this Fiona person. The man was exhausting to keep up with, and now he was her problem, not mine.

"You're a stronger woman than I am. I'm already hoping he takes a line drive to the nuts within minutes." Once on the first floor, we stepped through the employee exit into the late afternoon sun. "I want a full report on this Fiona person," Miriam added. "She probably doesn't hold a candle to you."

An outrageously flattering and completely baseless statement, but I appreciated the vote of confidence. "I doubt that's the case, but it doesn't matter. All I care about is if she can hold her own on the field, and from what Thomas said, that won't be an issue. Let's go back to your dinner with Devon. I hope he takes you some-place nice."

"Sugar plum fairies!" she exclaimed, pressing a hand to her forehead. "I didn't even ask what I should wear. What if it's super fancy and I'm underdressed? Or what if he takes me for burgers and I'm overdressed?"

I gave her a calming pat on the arm. "There's still time to ask. Just send a text on your way home. Or wear a cute little dress and flats. That would work no matter where he takes you."

"Yes, I can do that," she said, panic subsiding. "I'd better hurry so I don't miss the bus. Call me if you need me tonight. I'll answer no matter what."

I would not be interrupting her evening for any reason. "Don't worry about me. Just go have fun."

"I'm sending good thoughts your way," she said, blowing me a kiss as she veered off toward the bus stop, and I continued on to cross at Wabash and Neptune Street.

I told myself I didn't need those good thoughts, but the butterflies in my stomach said otherwise.

———

My apartment was four blocks from the library, mostly uphill on the way home, which provided my daily exercise. On days it rained I opted to drive, but taking the car such a short distance was pointless otherwise. If I'd have remembered the softball practice, I would have driven and brought my change of clothes. Now I had to hoof it even faster up the hill if I wanted to make it on time.

As I passed the post office, I couldn't help but think about Fletcher and his new girlfriend. How long had they been together? Did he meet her *before* dumping me? Did he dump me *because* of her? I had no reason to suspect he'd cheated, but my wayward thoughts were having a field day making up scenarios about clandestine meetings and the pair of them sexting while he and I watched television.

Why hadn't I asked Thomas *when* they started dating? *Because then you'd look even more pathetic than you already do*, I reminded myself. Bristling at the thought, my friend Lindsey's voice played through my head.

You are not pathetic, and you do not need that sorry excuse for a man.

I wished I could be as bold and confident as Lindsey was. All of my four best friends were more self-assured than I was, but Lindsey had chutzpah, as Grandma Ruth used to call it.

I rounded the corner onto Steuben Street and traveled the last half block as quickly as I could, my thighs burning like crazy. My building was easy to spot. Though a nondescript two-story house with beige siding was nothing to catch the eye, the overall appearance gave the impression that half of the structure was missing. It was the way the roof just ended on the left. Like something had once been there, but was now gone. The two doors pushed over to the far right were a nightmare for anyone who preferred symmetry, and the steps leading up to the porch were steep and uneven.

I landed here after the breakup with Fletcher. The

West End village wasn't the most posh part of town, but I liked being able to walk to work, and the upstairs apartment was one I could afford on my librarian salary, while also being a good size for the price. Thankfully, I had only the one neighbor downstairs and though nosy, August Banks—or Augie to his friends—was quiet and friendly and only occasionally complained that I made too much noise.

"There you are," said the neighbor in question, catching me as I unlocked my front door directly to the right of his. "Patrick put your mail in my box again. I'll remind him tomorrow to be more careful."

Why he needed to tell me this instead of simply putting the mail into my box I never knew. I secretly suspected that he fished envelopes out of my mailbox just to have an excuse to talk to me. He was sweet, but I didn't have time for a chat today.

"Thank you. I'm sure it was an honest mistake." I took the mail from his hand and pushed open my door. "I'd love to talk, but I'm in a hurry."

"Do you have a date?" he asked.

Amber eyes lit up as his bushy gray brows arched high, increasing the number of lines across his ebony forehead. For a man his age—which I guessed to be around seventy-five based on a story he once told about his high school days in the early sixties—he had impressive skin. Though wrinkles were inevitable, as they were for all of us at some point, he could pass for at least ten years younger than he was.

"Not a date. I have softball practice and I still have to change."

"Oh," he replied, his face falling. "I still say you and Patrick should go out. He's single, you know. A very nice young man."

Young being a relative term in this case. Yes, our letter carrier was young compared to Augie, but closer to my dad's age than mine.

"I really am in a hurry. I promise I'll come down and visit soon."

My phone dinged and I checked the screen to find a text from Fletcher. *Do you want a ride to practice?*

He could not be serious.

"What is it?" Augie asked. "Is everything all right?"

"Yes, it's fine," I assured him through clenched teeth. "Just a message I wasn't expecting. I'll talk to you tomorrow."

I rushed inside and up the stairs, dropping my purse and the mail onto the couch before firing off a succinct reply.

No.

Eight months without a single word, and now a text out of nowhere? Did he expect me to ride in the back while Fiona shot loving glances his way from the passenger seat? Not in this lifetime. I checked the screen again and fought the urge to add *but thank you* to my reply. Damn my good manners.

Instead, I tossed the cell onto the couch with the purse and raced into the bedroom to change, but I also needed to vent so I snatched the phone back up and called my friend Josie.

CHAPTER THREE

Putting the call on speaker, I dropped the cell on the bed and rummaged through my dresser.

"Hey, girl," Josie Danvers said, answering after the second ring, "what's up?"

The financial wizard of our group, Josie was the epitome of the girl next door. Thin, blond, educated, and successful. She could bake you cookies and then tell you how to set up your retirement portfolio while you ate them. My meager salary didn't leave much for savings, but she'd walked me through a basic, low-risk plan that would provide a nice living in another thirty-five to forty years.

"He sent me a text," I shouted. "He asked if I want a ride to practice."

Knowing exactly who *he* was, Josie replied, "What a shit. What did you tell him?"

"I told him no. What else was I supposed to say?"

"Where he could shove that ride," she said. "Are you sure you want to do this? You can always find another team to play on."

"If I change teams, he'll know why I did it. I won't give him the satisfaction." Plus, all the rosters would be filled for fall by now.

Josie made a harrumph sound before saying, "Sometimes happiness has to come before pride."

Jamming a foot into a pair of black leggings, I fell onto the bed and shoved in the other foot. "I found out he has a girlfriend."

"Oh, shit," she said in a whisper. "Hon—"

"She's on the team, too."

"Jesus, Megan, walk away. Who cares what he thinks? Some of my coworkers have a team this year. One phone call and I'll have you on the roster by tomorrow."

That was not going to happen. *This* was the team I'd been dying to be on for two years. *This* was the team everyone wanted to beat but no one wanted to play because they were that good. *This* was where I wanted to be, Fletcher or no Fletcher.

"I'm not quitting, Josie. I can't. Then he wins."

"For a nonconfrontational introvert, you have one hell of a competitive streak."

This wasn't about competition. Okay, maybe a little. But mostly, I had to get myself back again. At some point during the three years that Fletcher and I dated, I'd stopped being Megan and became Fletcher's girlfriend. When I walked into a party, people would say "Fletcher and his girlfriend are here." When I ran into one of his friends at the store, they'd say, "Hey, it's Fletcher's girlfriend." I never corrected them. I assumed this role of supporting character in the book of Fletcher Howard's life, and once he wrote me off the page, I didn't know who I was anymore.

But before I was Fletcher's girlfriend, I was a ballplayer. If I was going to find Megan again, this was the best place I knew to look.

"There's more to it than that," I said, slipping off my blouse and tossing it into the clothes hamper. I snagged a T-shirt from the dresser and tugged it on before grabbing the phone and hurrying into the bathroom. "This was my thing before I met Fletcher. I won't let him take it away from me."

He'd taken enough already.

"You're right," Josie said after a brief pause. "I just hate the way he treated you."

Fletcher was never mean. He didn't bully or make demands. He'd simply let me believe that he loved me just the way I am, and that turned out to be a lie.

"That's in the past," I said, brushing my hair up into a ponytail. "Being on the team with him isn't the greatest thing in the world, but it isn't the worst either."

"Let's hope you're still saying that once this practice is over." Whether I was or not, I'd just have to deal with whatever came my way, because quitting was not an option. "Call me after," Josie added. "I want a full report."

"We're having lunch tomorrow, remember? I'll share then."

Life had been more hectic than usual lately so the five of us were meeting to catch up on everyone's lives. Personally, I was most looking forward to hearing about Becca and her new man. They'd met back in May in the most random way possible, and she was blissfully in love to the point that she practically floated when she walked.

"Fine, I'll wait," she said as I carried her—via the phone—into the living room. "But if you need me tonight, I'm here."

Thank heaven for good friends. "I know."

Reaching the back of the couch, I grabbed my purse and caught a glimpse of an envelope with my name and address written in a handwriting I didn't recognize. The postmark was from San Francisco. Who would be writing to me from out there? Flipping it over, I found a return address scribbled in the top center and my heart stopped.

Geraldine Pendleton.

My mother's name. The mother I hadn't seen since I was seven years old.

"Megan?" Josie said through the phone. "What's wrong? Are you okay?"

I must have made a sound I was unaware of. "Yes, I'm fine. I just stubbed my toe." I didn't have the time or the mental fortitude to open the Pandora's box in my hand, and Josie would never let me ignore it if she knew what I was looking at. "I need to go or I'm going to be late. Thanks for letting me vent. I'll see you tomorrow."

"Wai—"

I ended the call and dropped the envelope back onto the couch before tossing the phone into my purse. Running on autopilot, I dragged my tennis shoes from the tiny closet near the door and slipped them on. Pretending the letter I'd dreamed about getting my whole life wasn't teetering on one of my throw pillows, I flung the purse onto my shoulder, collected my gear bag from the closet, and sprinted down the stairs.

———

I NEARLY TURNED around to go back for the letter three times on the way to practice. Why would my mother send me a letter now? What could she possibly have to say after pretending I didn't exist for more than two decades? Did she want forgiveness? Did she want a relationship? Did I? I was so distracted by the questions racing through my mind that I nearly missed the turn for Banksville Park. Hanging a quick left, I pushed the letter from my mind and braced for the trial ahead.

One ordeal at a time.

Spotting Fletcher's red Dodge Charger, I parked my gray Civic hatchback as far down the lot as possible.

He'd always wanted me to upgrade to something more exciting. Something bright and sporty. Even my car was boring in Fletcher's opinion.

Shading my eyes from the late-day sun, I peered over the players warming up on the field. The Banksville Bombers. I couldn't believe I'd finally made the team. Players were paired up, tossing the ball back and forth, and I hoped I could find someone still available to warm up with.

Without knowing the full roster, I couldn't be sure how many teammates I already knew, but there were definitely a few familiar faces, most of whom I knew through Fletcher. Then I spotted Roxanne, who I'd played with on two teams before and breathed a sigh of relief. She was tall, sweet, and had been the only person who messaged me kind words of support after the breakup.

I'd been too upset to play the spring season, and no one except Roxanne seemed to notice my absence.

Opening my hatch, I reached in for my gear bag and forgot that the hydraulics that kept the door up weren't what they used to be. With a thud, hard plastic smacked the back of my skull. I was still seeing stars when a voice said, "Are you okay?"

Startled, I spun around and inadvertently slammed the bag, bat end first, into the stranger's stomach. He doubled over with an oomph.

"I'm so sorry," I said, dropping the bag onto the pavement. "I didn't realize you were so close." I bent to see his face. "Can you breathe? I'm really sorry."

The man held up a hand but remained bent over. "I'm good. Just give me a second."

If this was a stranger, I'd just made a horrible first impression. All I could see was black hair curling around the edges of a ball cap so I wasn't sure if I knew him or not.

"Okay," he said, straightening and rubbing a hand over his sternum. I definitely didn't know him. "If you swing a bat as well as you swing that bag, we're going to have a good season." Lips slanted into a grin as he extended a hand. "I'm Ryan Stallings. Sorry I scared you like that."

Accepting the greeting, I tried not to stare, but he was so cute I couldn't help it. His eyes were the color of aged whiskey and surrounded by the longest lashes I'd ever seen on a man. A barely-there five-o'clock shadow covered his narrow jawline, and the grin revealed a perfect row of white teeth. At five foot two, I was used to being towered over, but that wasn't the case with this man. I guessed him to be maybe five eight or nine, and his hand was soft and warm against mine.

"Megan Knox," I said, amazed I was able to get the two words past my lips. Speaking of lips, his were utterly perfect. Full and smooth and distractingly kissable. "I'm late."

Ryan shook his head. "Practice doesn't start for another five minutes so we're both on time."

"Oh. Right." I retrieved my bag from the ground and lifted it onto my shoulder. "I don't usually like to cut it so close, but I forgot to take a change of clothes to work." As if my brain and mouth had disengaged, I continued to babble. "Luckily, the traffic wasn't too bad on the way here. Did you hit traffic?"

Why couldn't I make my mouth shut up?

"I live in Greentree so it wasn't bad." Pointing to the field, he said, "Looks like we might be the last two. You want to warm up?"

I nearly said no for fear I'd get too distracted staring at his face and take a ball to the nose. Unable to come up with an excuse that wouldn't reveal my odd instant crush or come off sounding rude, I accepted. "Sure."

We walked together in silence across the outfield to the third base bench. Dropping our bags, we both pulled out our gloves and Ryan said, "I'll get a ball from the bucket and meet you in left."

Nodding, I trotted onto the field and spotted Roxanne twenty yards away. She was warming up with a man I didn't know. To her left were Fletcher and a woman I assumed to be Fiona. If so, Miriam's assumption had been very wrong. The woman was an African goddess with the body of an Olympic athlete turned supermodel. I, on the other hand, was a pasty garden gnome with childbearing hips and knobby knees.

Making Fiona a considerable upgrade.

This personal assessment did not come from a lack of self-esteem. I was cute in a *Are you old enough to be in this bar?* kind of way. When I was forty people would still assume I was barely out of college, which had its advantages. But there were times when I wished I looked like a grown woman. One with a swanlike neck, legs that went on for days, and an innate sophistication that made men want to be in my orbit.

Like Fiona.

"You ready?" asked Ryan, startling me once again. I really needed to cut back on that afternoon cup of coffee.

"I am." I jogged toward the outfield fence to put some distance between us and held up my glove. "Fire away."

Three tosses later, I was relieved to know I wasn't nearly as rusty as I'd feared. Keeping my focus on the ball and not the couple forty yards over proved more difficult than I liked, but Ryan's smile helped. Since I knew little about him besides his name and the fact he lived in Greentree, I forced myself not to get carried away. He could have a girlfriend or a wife. Or a husband for that matter.

Plus, I'd already done the *date a fellow player* thing and look how that turned out. Did I want to try that again?

"Come on in!" came a voice from in front of home plate as the ball landed in my glove.

Everyone headed for the infield, and as I stepped

from grass to dirt, Fletcher appeared next to me. "Hey there."

Elated and annoyed and annoyed that I was elated, I kept my eyes straight ahead. "Hi."

"I'm glad you're here. I was afraid you might not play."

"Why wouldn't I?" I asked, genuinely curious what he would say.

"Well…" he hedged. "You know."

Stopping, I turned his way. "No, I don't know. Why wouldn't I play, Fletcher?" He knew how much I loved softball, and he knew how badly I'd wanted to be on this team. Did he really think I'd give up everything just to avoid seeing his stupid face? This was exactly why I *had* to play.

Eyes wide, he remained silent.

"Gather around so we can sort out positions," said Barry Brownhurst, the man who had coached this team to the league championship six years running.

No longer interested in whatever Fletcher might say, I walked away and joined the others. I didn't come here to fight with Fletcher. I came to play ball. And that's what I planned to do.

CHAPTER FOUR

"Most of you have either played for me or played on teams I've coached against, so I assigned positions we can start with. It's only the first practice so there's time to switch and make adjustments if needed."

Coach Barry was nothing if not efficient. He didn't take the game so seriously that no one had fun—that's why we were playing, after all—but he approached the season with an intention to win and demanded that his players do the same. I'd played against teams in the past who preferred to drink and laugh and for them winning or losing didn't matter. That was their prerogative. It wasn't as if we were playing for money in these adult leagues. Personally, I stepped on the field to compete, and I liked to play with teammates who did the same.

"Stallings," he said, addressing Ryan, "You're the

only one I don't know, but I understand you play shortstop?"

"Yes, sir," Ryan nodded. "All-state in high school and then on through my years at U of Akron."

A quiet murmur hummed through the team. We rarely got anyone with even these minor accomplishments.

"Then you'll start there today. Howard on first, Knox on second, and Carpelli on third," Coach flipped the sheet atop his clipboard as I groaned internally. It was one thing to play on the same team, but I'd forgotten that Fletcher and I played positions next to each other. "Derby on the mound and Wang behind the plate. The rest of you spread out in the outfield for now."

We took the positions assigned and to my surprise, Fletcher drifted over my way. "That was arrogant what I said earlier. Just forget it, okay?"

Why did my opinion matter to him so much? It wasn't as if we'd stayed friends. Not that we were enemies either, but friends didn't kick you out of their apartment and then pretend you no longer existed for the next eight months.

"There's nothing to forget," I said. "Let's focus on playing and leave the past where it belongs."

I nearly patted myself on the back for such a grown-up response, considering I really wanted to tell him where he could shove this sudden nice act. He nodded and shuffled over to first base.

For the next half hour, Coach Barry hit the ball around the field and we all adjusted to working together. Ryan had a stellar arm and we quickly fell into a rhythm, taking turns covering the bag. I only missed one throw and that was because he smiled at me and my brain went all gooey. Fiona had backed me up and got the ball back in with a long soaring throw from center field to home plate. Did she have to be gorgeous *and* that good?

The temperature was still high despite it being mid-September, and by the time Coach gave us a water break, I had sweat in places that I didn't want to think about.

"You're good," Ryan said, falling into step beside me. "Did you play in college?"

"I played *while* in college, but not for the school team," I replied, flattered that he asked. "I wasn't good enough to make it at Penn State."

He filled a small cup from the water cooler and held it out for me to take. Quite the gentlemanly move. "What do you do when you aren't snagging grounders out of the dirt?"

"I'm a…"

This was an important moment. Telling a man what I did for a living often resulted in them immediately pegging me for boring, and the conversation ended there. I didn't want this conversation to end, so I bent the truth.

"I work in a bookstore."

Bookstore gave off a hipster image, or so I thought.

Like I wore cool, dime-store clothes, drank a lot of coffee, and listened to deep, indie music. My clothes often came from thrift stores, but I drank more tea than coffee, and I couldn't remember the last time I listened to anything other than an audiobook. Ryan didn't need to know all that yet. If this went anywhere, I could always confess the truth once he got to know me.

"One of the big chains?" he asked.

I shook my head. "No, a small independent. You probably haven't heard of it. What do you do?"

He was filling another cup so I couldn't see his face when he said, "I… help people with finances."

So he was in my friend Josie's field. "Like a broker or a financial planner?"

"Closer to the second."

We stepped away to give others access to the cooler, and I expected him to find someone else to talk to, but he stayed by my side. Leaning close, he lowered his voice and said, "Do you know everyone on the team?"

"Not all of them," I replied. "The guy in the plain black cap, and that one over there with the sunglasses on the back of his neck are new to me." Remembering I'd just met *him* today, I added, "And you, of course."

"I moved to town at the start of the year so I don't know a lot of people. That's why I agreed to play."

"How did you get on this team?" I asked. I'd been trying for four years and only got the call this summer.

"An old college buddy was on the team, but he moved to DC a couple of months ago. He gave my name as his replacement."

Looking around, I said, "Was that Mike Klumski?"

Ryan's brown eyes went wide. "How did you know?"

"I've been playing either with or against these people for the last eight years. Mike is the only one missing, and he's so good I knew they'd never cut him from the line-up." Fletcher, Fiona, and I, plus the two men I didn't know, were the only other players who hadn't been on the team the previous year. "This is the hardest team to get on so you got lucky."

He sipped his water before saying, "Is that going to make me unpopular? I didn't know I might be taking someone else's spot."

"If you can play, then no one will care."

"Time for batting practice," called Coach Barry. "Everyone, take your positions and we'll start with the outfielders. Roxanne, you're up."

"Back to work," Ryan said, taking my empty cup and walking both his and mine to the garbage can several feet from the bench. The gesture made me smile, but then he was probably just a considerate person and I needed to stop acting like a preteen getting noticed by the cutest boy in school.

Grabbing my glove, I jogged onto the field. Once I reached my position, I turned to see Fletcher talking to Ryan by the bench. Words were exchanged, and then

Ryan held up his hands right before Fletcher walked away. What the heck was that about?

I would have asked, but Coach yelled for us to be ready, and Priscilla Derby wound up to pitch. I glanced over to Ryan, but he had his glove down and his eyes on the batter. Something felt off. I had no reason to assume that the new guy was interested in anything beyond making a friend, but he was cute and nice and if Fletcher had a problem with me talking to him, he needed to get over it.

His right to an opinion on anything I did ended eight months ago. That had been *his* choice, not mine, but I'd learned to live with it and he needed to do the same.

———

The rest of the practice was uneventful, and as we all walked off to pack up, I couldn't help but notice that Ryan kept his distance. What the heck did Fletcher say to him?

"Drinks at Alexion's?" said Jeremy Wang as he removed his catcher's gear.

"Yes, please," chimed in Dalton Minx, an outfielder and one of the best hitters on the team. I'd played with him several years before and remembered him as a laid-back guy who never took anything too seriously. Except when he stepped into the batter's box.

All of the teams I'd played on had a regular watering

hole they frequented, typically at a bar close to their main practice field. The Bombers had been going to Alexion's, a family-owned bar that had been around since the 1950s, for as long as I could remember. I'd been there on a couple of occasions with friends, but never during ball season.

"Not me," Theresa Carpelli said. "The hubby has to work early in the morning so I'm on bath and bedtime duty for the kids."

"I can stay for about an hour." Priscilla tossed a ball into the five-gallon bucket beside the bench. "How about you, new guy?"

Everyone looked at Ryan, who was silently stuffing his glove into his bag. When he noticed the attention, he looked up and said, "Me?"

"Yeah," she said. "Are you coming?"

I didn't know Priscilla well, though I did know she wasn't married. Maybe I wasn't the only one who'd found Ryan attractive.

Ryan shook his head. "Sorry, I need to get home."

"Well, I'm in." Roxanne bumped me with her elbow. "How about you, Megan?"

I wasn't much of a drinker, and knowing what was waiting for me at home, I opted to skip this one. "Not tonight."

A few others gave their replies, and we all made our way to the parking lot. I considered cornering Fletcher to ask what stunt he'd pulled with Ryan, but if whatever was said had nothing to do with me, I'd look like an arrogant fool.

"Hi," said a voice from my right when I reached the middle of the outfield. I looked up to find Fiona smiling down at me.

"Hello."

"I'm Fiona Lewis."

Keeping my face expressionless, I said, "I know."

Seconds passed in an awkward silence before she said, "I don't want this to be weird."

Too late, but I played along. "Want what to be weird?"

"Us. I know you were with Fletcher for a while and now I'm with Fletcher and we're on the same team…" she trailed off.

I couldn't help but wonder what Fletcher had told her about our breakup. About me. Pride kept me from asking.

"I don't have a problem if you don't," I lied.

Fiona visibly relaxed. "Oh, good. You're like a legend around here, and I was so afraid you'd hate me on sight."

A legend? Since when?

"I have no reason to hate you." As far as I knew, anyway. "Fletcher and I broke up months ago. He's free to date whoever he wants, just like I am."

As if we were suddenly girlfriends, she leaned close and dropped her voice to a whisper. "I saw you talking to the new guy. He's cute."

Not hating her didn't mean I wanted to be besties. I

also didn't trust that Fletcher wasn't using her to find out what I thought of Ryan. "He seems nice." We reached the parking lot and I added, "Have fun at the bar."

"I can't go tonight. I've got a family thing. But I'll see you at the next practice."

I'd expected her to ride with Fletcher, but she walked on to a black Jeep a few spots past my car. "Have a good night," I called.

After popping my hatch, careful this time not to let it close on me, I looked around for Ryan but he was nowhere in sight. He hadn't said a word to me since the water break, and I was certain that Fletcher must have interfered. Something he had no right to do.

Dropping into my driver's seat, I huffed and wondered why men had to be so annoying. Then I shoved the key into the ignition and mumbled, "If I knew the answer to that one, I'd share it with every woman ever and save us all the trouble."

———

TRUDGING up the stairs to my apartment, I felt as if I were dragging a boulder along with me. I slid my bag into the closet, kicked off my shoes, and went into the kitchen to find food. I should have been starving since there hadn't been time to eat before practice, but nothing sounded good. I definitely didn't want to cook, and there were no leftovers in the fridge that I could quickly heat up.

Checking the pantry, I stared at the shelves for several seconds before making an emotional decision I would probably regret later, but tonight called for chocolate frosting and a large spoon. Treat in hand, I took a seat on the couch and stared at the letter teetering on my lemon-yellow throw pillow. The letter stared back, taunting me.

You know you want to read me. You know you do.

I flipped the pillow to hide the envelope and scooped a heaping serving of frosting into my mouth. "I never asked you to send me a ledder," I said with my mouth full.

Two bites later, I picked up the phone and called the person this letter affected the most. Other than me, of course. Dad picked up on the third ring.

"Hey, pumpkin. Is everything okay?"

I didn't normally call him when he was at his convention. Dad started selling insurance around the time I went to kindergarten, and every September he attended his company gathering, which changed locations every year. This time they were in Dallas.

"I'm good. How's it going down there?" I asked, not ready to admit my reason for calling.

"It's good. Really good." Someone spoke in the background and he mumbled a response I couldn't make out. "Some of us are chatting in the bar. Let me step out so I can hear you."

The notion of Dad in a bar did not compute, but then this wasn't some seedy dive on the North Side. He was at a Hyatt Regency, after all. There was a shuffling sound, a couple of excuse mes, and then he said, "Okay, I'm out in the lobby now. What's going on?"

I never meant for him to think this was an emergency. Though, was it? Did hearing from your mother for the first time in two decades require a 911 call to the parent who'd been there the whole time? And if I told him about said letter, would this ruin the rest of his trip? Knowing Dad, he'd insist on coming home immediately. I didn't want that. This trip was his one annual indulgence. I would not let Geraldine Pendleton take that away from him. She'd already taken enough from both of us.

"I had my first practice of the season tonight," I said, regretting making the call. "I know most of the team, and the coach put me at second base right away."

Between my height—or lack thereof— and my gender, I'd had to fight for my position on more than one team over the years. It had been nice to not face that fight this time.

"That's great, pumpkin. They should all know how good you are by now."

He was my dad. He had to say that.

"How did your presentation go? Or have you given it yet?"

"That was today and it went well. Everyone in attendance left knowing more about the Schedule P Reserve than they probably wanted to. And no one fell asleep this time."

I loved my dad, but even his colleagues found his fascination with all things insurance a little odd. He'd found what made him happy and I loved that for him.

"Now are you going to tell me the real reason you called?" he asked, as clairvoyant as ever. Anyone who said only moms had that intuition thing hadn't been raised by James Knox.

I went with a half-truth. "I got something in the mail today that I wanted to talk to you about, but it can wait until you get back."

"Is it an insurance matter?"

"No, it's something else. Nothing important." This was quite possibly the first lie I'd ever told my father.

He didn't respond, and I feared he'd push for more details. "Are you sure? I have plenty of time to talk."

As if on cue, I heard someone call his name before he said, "We're at a table in the back corner on the left. Go on in." To me, he said, "I can go up to my room where it's quieter."

Dad had no social life outside of work, and I would not take these rare moments away from him. "Really, it's fine. Go have fun with your friends, and I'll see you when you get back. Your flight lands at three thirty, right?"

"Unless there's a delay. If you change your mind, you can call anytime. I might not answer right away if I'm in a panel, but I'll call back as soon as I can."

A girl couldn't ask for a better dad. I considered throwing the letter away and pretending it never came, but the curiosity would drive me crazy. I *would* read it, but not alone. Not without him.

"It can wait a couple more days; don't worry. Go back to your friends and have a good time. I'll see you on Sunday."

"Love you, pumpkin."

"Love you, too, Dad."

The call ended and I dropped the phone next to my leg before going back to my frosting. This had been one eventful day. First the threat to the programs, then the letter, and whatever that was with Ryan at practice. This was not typical for my life. I was used to maybe one mildly interesting event a couple of times a year.

Like Becca getting a second chance at love. Or a bestselling author making an appearance at the library. Yes, I gave both of those events equal billing because Becca had been through hell when she'd lost the love of her life two years ago, and seeing her happy again was better than all the bestselling authors in the world.

Two more bites of frosting and I carried the container back to the kitchen and put it in the fridge before heading to the bathroom for a much-needed shower. Sleep would not be a problem tonight. On my way through the living room, I stopped and checked under the throw pillow, silently hoping the letter would be gone. No luck. I had the fleeting thought that a warning should be printed on the outside.

Danger—may turn life of recipient upside down.

After shoving the letter into my purse, I grabbed my phone and shuffled into the bedroom for my pajamas. The potential time bomb would have to wait, and so would the woman who sent it.

CHAPTER FIVE

WHEN I'D MADE MY LIST OF CURVEBALLS FROM THE previous day, I'd forgotten about Fletcher's text message and odd behavior. Josie had not forgotten.

"What happened at practice?" she asked before my butt hit the seat of my chair. "Did he try to talk to you?"

"He who?" said Donna as she joined us. "Are we talking about Fletch the Wretch?"

She'd given him that moniker within a week of our breakup. Donna Bradford was a force of nature. A photographer and leading female entrepreneur, she made a living shooting weddings, but her passion was in using her art for racial activism. As a biracial woman, she understood the struggle in a way the rest in our group never would.

"Wait until the others get here," I said. "I don't want to tell this story more than once."

What I didn't say was that the letter burning a hole through my purse was a much bigger deal than my ex sending me a text message, but I still hadn't decided if I was going to tell them about it or not. With anything else, I wouldn't hesitate, but a part of me felt like it was wrong to tell them before I told Dad. Then again, keeping it from them would be weird. We told each other everything.

The waitress took our orders while we waited. We'd eaten together so many times that each of us could have ordered for the others and never gotten it wrong. As the server walked away, Becca and Lindsey arrived.

"Sorry we're late," Becca said. "Lindsey tried to break the sound barrier on the way here, and we got pulled over."

"You what?" Donna said.

Lindsey waved a hand as if this was no big deal. "I got a warning. And I was not trying to *break the sound barrier*. I was only going twelve miles per hour over the speed limit."

"Where?" Josie asked.

"On the Parkway," Becca replied as she unfolded her napkin and spread it across her lap. "We were talking and she was so oblivious, we didn't even know the cop was chasing us until we reached the top of the Greentree exit."

"Can we move on?" Lindsey chimed. "I didn't get a ticket. We're all here now. Let's eat."

Mendoza's was Lindsey's favorite Mexican restaurant. We took turns picking the meeting place, and she always chose this one. None of us minded since they had the best huevos rancheros in town, which they served any time of day.

"Yes," Josie said. "Let's move on. Megan, spill."

"What is she spilling?" Becca asked.

With a sigh, I said, "Fletcher sent me a text message before practice yesterday asking if I wanted a ride."

Lindsey loaded guacamole onto a corn chip. "Please tell me that was a literal question and not a euphemism."

"Literal," I replied. "I haven't heard from him in nearly eight months, and less than an hour before the message came, I found out that he has a new girlfriend."

"Oh, Meg," Becca said, patting my hand.

"She's on the team, too," I added.

"That peckerhead." Donna dropped her chip on her appetizer plate and brushed her hands together. "Did he know that you knew?"

Excellent question and one I hadn't thought of. "I have no idea. Thomas told me at work, and he'd assumed I knew, but I'm not sure how I would have. I don't associate with many of our mutual friends anymore so I'm out of the loop."

The truth was that they had been Fletcher's friends and once we were no longer together, most of them had dumped me as well. Which was fine. I had all the friends I needed right here.

"You didn't take the ride, did you?" Lindsey asked.

"Of course not. I told him no."

"Just no?" Donna said. "Not *hell no, you boil on the butt of humanity*?"

"You know she'd never say that." Becca dabbed at her chin with her napkin. "Do you want me to have Jacob beat him up for you?"

The question was so ridiculous that we all laughed. "I appreciate the offer," I said, "but there's no need to get your boyfriend an assault charge on my behalf."

"He'd do it," she added. "I'm pretty sure you're his favorite in this group."

"Hey," the other three protested.

"I'm the one who helped him rework that 401K," Josie argued.

"I'm the one who took those pictures of the two of you before he left for Korea back in July," Donna said. "For free, I might add."

"Those pictures were for your exhibit," Becca reminded her. "And Megan is the one Sophie loves, so she's Jacob's favorite."

Sophie was Jacob's six-year-old daughter from his previous marriage. She was beautiful, smart, and loved to read. As a librarian who spent a great deal of time with children her age, I'd brought along a collection of books the first time we all met her, and she and I had bonded immediately. Sophie didn't like me more than she liked Becca, but I could tell that I was a close second.

News to me that I'd won her father over as well.

"I appreciate the offer, but no thanks. At least not yet." I still wanted to know what Fletcher said to Ryan. If he pulled some 'stay away from her' crap, then I wanted to keep my options open. "At practice he said he was glad I decided to play. I think he wants to be friends."

"And I want chocolate cake that won't go to my hips," Donna said. "We can't all have what we want."

"Do you *want* to be friends with him?" Becca asked.

"You can't be friends with an ex," Lindsey said before stuffing another chip in her mouth. Four sets of eyes turned her way and she caught the stares with a wide-eyed look. "What? It's true. If you could be friends, then you wouldn't have broken up in the first place."

"Aren't you still friends with Zach Dugan?" Josie asked.

"And Robbie Winters," Becca added.

Lindsey shook her head. "Those don't count."

The rest of us exchanged confused glances. "Why don't they count?" I asked.

"Because I was never serious about those guys. I never considered marrying either of them."

Josie lifted her glass. "You practically lived with Zach when we were in college. Don't even try to pretend you weren't hearing wedding bells when he took you to meet his parents."

"In the *Hamptons*," Josie added.

"That's when I knew we would never get married,"

Lindsey said. "A girl from Carnegie was never going to be good enough for the Dugans of West Chester."

Becca tapped her shoulder. "Then you *did* think about marrying him."

"Please," she said, loading up another chip. "He was awful in bed. I would not have signed up for a lifetime of that." We all had a guy from college who fit that description, and an understanding nod went around the table. "Now can we get back to Megan's story?"

"So you met the girlfriend?" Donna asked.

"Wait, she didn't answer my question," Becca cut in. "Do you want to be friends with Fletcher?"

If asked the same question back when the breakup first happened, I might have said yes. Today, I wouldn't even consider it. "No, I don't. And yes, I met Fiona."

"Fiona?" Josie repeated. "That's a heck of a name."

"And she's a heck of a woman." I glanced over to Donna. "If you need a new model, she's your girl. Perfect bone structure, beautiful black skin, and those green eyes that most of us could only dream of. She has to be pushing six feet tall, and Thomas says she played softball for Duquesne. Yesterday she hurled a ball from center field to home plate without a single bounce. She's that good."

"Please tell me she isn't nice, too," Josie said.

She was going to be disappointed. "She caught me after practice to introduce herself and said she hoped I didn't hate her. Which I don't. It isn't as if he dumped me *for her.*" I'd finally put that concern to rest by dropping my pride enough to message Thomas and ask how long Fletcher and Fiona had been together. He'd said about three months.

The waitress arrived with our drinks and everyone put in their orders, including a request from Lindsey for a refill on the corn chips. As the young woman walked away, Donna started talking about her neighbor moving out. She'd set him up with Becca back in May, and the date had not gone well. That had been before Becca met Jacob.

Technically, they'd already met, but only as passing strangers who kept running into each other in weird situations. Jacob and Becca's love story was one of serendipity and fate, and maybe a little divine intervention. Becca's high school sweetheart had been killed in a horrible tragedy the day before their wedding so there was a good chance Brian was up there working hard to make sure she still got her happily ever after. If not with him, then with someone else who would love her the way she deserved.

I tuned out in the middle of the story about the neighbor getting his massive gym equipment stuck in the stairwell. Staring at my water glass, my mind drifted to the letter in my purse. Dad had once told me how he fell in love with my mother the moment he'd met her. The girl he'd described had been bright and beautiful and loved to dance. As a young girl, I remembered feeling overwhelmed by the force of her presence. She would dress me up and put on music so we could dance around the house, but I'd always asked to go back to my room to read.

Maybe if I'd known she was going to leave us, I'd have made more of an effort to be the dazzling, outgoing daughter that she'd wanted. Not that I hadn't tried. Geraldine had been a hard woman to please, and I paid the price anytime I failed to do so.

"Hey," said Josie, snapping her fingers in front of my face. "Earth to Megan."

I looked up to find all eyes on me. "I'm sorry. How did they get the weight thing off the stairs?"

Lindsey snorted as Becca said, "She finished that story two minutes ago. What's going on with you, Meg?"

I hesitated, but these were my people. I had to share. Reaching for my purse, I pulled out the letter and tossed it onto the table. "I got this yesterday."

Josie picked it up first. "What is it?" Turning it over, she asked, "Who is Geraldine Pendleton?"

"That's my mother." The words felt foreign on my tongue. I couldn't remember the last time I'd said them. "As you all know, I haven't heard from her since she sent me a card for my tenth birthday."

"It's still sealed," Lindsey mumbled around a chip. "Are you going to open it?"

I told myself that I was waiting for Dad to get back, but part of me didn't want to tell him. I didn't know if what was in that envelope would hurt him. Or hurt me, for that matter. Was there an apology? An explanation? What if she needed money? I knew without a second thought that Dad would send her some. I didn't have much to spare, but my gut said I wouldn't give her anything no matter what was in my account. A childish, selfish thought, but too many years had gone by. Too many milestones missed. Moments when I'd needed a mom and she wasn't there.

Not that Dad hadn't been the best parent ever, but there were moments in a girl's life that only a mother could understand.

"I decided to wait until Dad gets back from his trip. It feels like something we should do together."

"What do you think she wants?" Becca asked.

I shrugged. "I have no idea. A million different scenarios have been running through my head, but it could be anything, I guess."

"She could be sick," Becca suggested.

"Or broke," Donna added.

The latter had occurred to me but not the former.

"What if she's coming back to town?" Lindsey licked salsa off her finger. "Or maybe she's already here."

Josie flipped the envelope again. "The postmark is from San Francisco."

"She could have mailed it before she left."

"Surely she'd give her more warning than that."

"Guys," I cut in, "we can sit here and guess all day, but there's no way to know until I open it."

Handing it back to me, Josie said, "When does your dad get back?"

"I pick him up at the airport tomorrow afternoon."

A silence fell over the table until Becca said, "Whatever it is, we're here for you. You know that, right?"

Yes, I did. I nodded and slid the letter into my purse. "Enough about me today. What's going on with the rest of you?"

"I've got nothing personal, but the exhibit is moving along," Donna said as the waitress returned with our orders.

As the food was laid out around the table, Josie's fajitas sizzled and Lindsey made a moaning sound as she sniffed her huevos rancheros. We dug in as Lindsey shared how the new school year was going, and Josie went on about a coworker who wouldn't stop making some sort of fish dish in the break room microwave. They had yet to discover the culprit, but apparently the entire office was on the case and no one was above suspicion.

I scooped up a bite of my burrito and locked eyes with Becca. She and I had been roommates in college and though all of us were close, she and I had a special bond. Probably because we were the two introverts of the group. The look spoke volumes and I understood the message loud and clear. She was thinking along the same lines I was. Whatever was in that letter probably wasn't going to be good.

"Are you going to eat those beans?" Lindsey asked, pulling me from my thoughts.

"You can have them." I scooped the refried beans onto an entree plate as Donna shared the latest news on her exhibition.

For the rest of the meal, I forced myself to stay in the moment. These were the important women in my life. The ones I knew would always be there for me. The one who existed only in an unopened letter didn't deserve more attention than they did.

CHAPTER SIX

DESPITE A THUNDERSTORM ROLLING THROUGH THE middle of the country, Dad's flight landed on time. Due to an accident on 376, I did not. Swooping in as another car pulled out, I put the car in park and hopped out to open the hatch.

"I'm so sorry," I said as he lifted the suitcase into the car. "Two lanes were closed on the interstate."

Dad kissed me on the cheek. "No problem, pumpkin. I haven't been out here long."

Average height, slender build, and receding hairline, James Knox had a smile that could charm a snake into buying snow skis. He was quiet and quite possibly the least threatening person on the planet, but that was his secret weapon. No one saw him coming. He wore dark-rimmed glasses with lenses thick enough to magnify his dark-brown eyes. They also made him look smart, which he was.

When I'd fallen behind in my math classes back in junior high, we hadn't bothered with tutors. Dad spent extra time with me every night until I'd brought my grade up to an A plus. When I'd struggled with physics my senior year of high school, he'd found every online video available and by the end of the semester, he could have passed the exam as well as I could.

He never embarrassed me because I loved his enthusiasm and his endless supply of positivity. Even when he'd asked my friends goofy questions or warned my dates that he may look harmless but he knew people who knew people that wouldn't like his little girl getting hurt. Dad was my hero, my mentor, and the best man I would ever find.

Which was why I hated to even bring up the letter. Geraldine had hurt him as much, if not more, than she'd hurt me. I'd always assumed she was the reason he never dated or remarried. Not that I ever asked him about dating, or his lack thereof. By the time I was fifteen, even I'd grown tired of people asking him why he hadn't found a mother for me yet.

As if those were sold in stores. Or a man couldn't possibly raise a little girl on his own. Despite the insulting questions, Dad had kept a smile on his face and never let it get to him.

"How was the flight?" I asked.

"We got out of Dallas late so I had to run to make the connection in St. Louis, but we left on time from there."

"Are you hungry?"

"I am, but if you've already eaten you don't have to stop."

I'd had a late breakfast and not eaten since. "I skipped lunch, actually. Do you want to stop somewhere in Robinson?" This was the large shopping area on the way back into town from the airport.

Trying not to sound too excited, Dad said, "I could go for some Eat'n Park." I knew when I asked that this would be his answer. The man loved Eat'n Park.

"Then Eat'n Park it will be."

Less than ten minutes later, we were seated in a small booth against a window, our order in—since we both got the same thing every time—and I debated whether this was a good time to bring up the letter. The night before I had the thought that maybe what was inside was important. What if she had some medical issue that could eventually affect me and she'd wanted me to know? Or what if she'd come into some money and decided—out of guilt or regret or both—to send me some.

I'd give it to Dad, of course. He'd never gone after child support and she'd never offered. Something I was unaware of until the subject of paying for my college had come up. Not only had he raised me with no assistance from the woman who gave birth to me, but he'd managed to set up a college fund that had made it possible for me to graduate debt free.

If Geraldine needed to pay anyone back, it was Dad.

"I have something to talk to you about," I said after the waitress delivered our drinks—mine a milkshake and Dad's a Cherry Coke.

"I need to talk to you about something, too," he said. The smile of pure joy on his face said his was good news so I let him go first.

"What is it?"

"You can go first." He was trying and failing to hide his grin.

"Not with that look on your face. What happened? Did you get a big promotion or something?"

Dad shook his head. "This isn't about work." Leaning his elbows on the table, he said, "Well, there's a connection, but it isn't that."

Now I was really curious. "Tell me already. What is it?"

Twirling the straw in his glass, he looked out the window and cleared his throat. Squirming in his seat, he finally clasped his hands on the table and said, "I'm not sure how you're going to take this."

Crap. They were transferring him. There had been the threat in the past, but he'd always managed to convince his higher-ups that he needed to stay in Pittsburgh. If he was happy about it, then I would be, too. Unless he was moving out of the country. I'd have a really hard time pretending to be happy about something like that.

"It's clearly good news so I'm sure I'll be happy about it." Another white lie. I was dropping those way too easily this weekend.

"Okay." Sitting up, he crossed his arms, then uncrossed them and cleared his throat again. "Here it goes. I'm seeing someone."

My brain went blank. "You're what?"

He grabbed my hand across the table. "I know this is a surprise. It surprised me, too. Nessa and I have known each other for years, and—"

"Nessa?" I repeated. Like the imaginary sea creature?

"Vanessa, actually. Vanessa Broneicki, but she goes by Nessa. She works in accounting, and we got to know each other while on the bowling team together this summer."

My gut reaction was to be happy for him. Or it would be once the shock wore off. This was all I'd ever wanted. Okay, not always. There had been a time when I'd feared he'd meet a woman with two mean daughters who would make my life miserable.

I might have watched too many Disney movies as a kid.

But other than that, I wanted him to find love again. I guess I just never thought it would happen after all this time.

"Is she nice?" I asked, unable to think of anything better to say. "What's she like?"

"She's two years older than I am and has two daughters." My worst fears were coming true. "One lives in New York City, and the other lives here in town with her husband and their little boy."

Wow. Built in grandkids. I hadn't even thought of that. Dad had been barely eighteen when I was born, and my mother had been seventeen. They'd gone to high school together in Uniontown, which was where I'd spent my first eighteen years until going off to college. My existence was the result of two kids getting carried away in the back seat of a Chevy Cavalier. Not the most auspicious start to life, but they'd married and started their little family.

Seven years later, my mother had decided that domestic life was not for her. That *we* were not for her. She'd taken off for California, and we'd picked up the pieces.

At this point, I had no idea what to say. What I knew for sure was that we would *not* be discussing the letter today. He was happy. He was finally moving on. Dragging up the past in the form of the woman who broke his heart and abandoned the both of us would only ruin his newfound joy.

A wave of fierceness rose in my chest. I would not let her hurt him again.

"How long has this been going on?" I asked. "Can I meet her?"

"She's dying to meet you." The waitress arrived with our food so we paused until she walked away. Spreading the butter on his pancakes, Dad said, "Our first real date was two months ago, but like I said, we've known each other for a long time."

I reached for the ketchup. "Dad, I'm so happy to hear this. I can't believe you didn't mention her sooner."

"Like I said, I wasn't sure how you'd take it."

"If I ever gave you the impression that I didn't want you to be happy—"

"No, honey, that isn't it." He set the small pitcher of syrup down beside his plate. "It's been just the two of us for a long time. Bringing someone else into the picture felt… well… I just wasn't sure if we were ready for that."

We'd had plenty of time to be ready. "Dad, it's been over twenty years. Please tell me you haven't stayed single all this time because of me."

"Goodness, no. I mean, when you were little I didn't want to bring someone into your life that might not…" He trailed off so I finished the sentence for him.

"Stick around?"

"Yes," he said, his shoulders dropping. "After what happened with—"

"That was a long time ago," I said, cutting him off. "Today is about you and Nessa and if the look on your face when you talk about her is any indication, she makes you really happy. That's all that matters."

The smile returned. Not as bright as before, but almost there. What happened in the past was still a wound for him. One I would never reopen for anything.

"Enough about me," he said, slicing into a pancake. "What was your news?"

I needed a story and fast, but nothing came to mind. Reaching, I said, "I was thinking about looking at new cars."

"Really?" he said, glancing up from his food. "I thought you wanted to go without a car payment for a while."

Yes, I did. Which was why I wasn't at all thinking about new cars. "You're right. It's a bad idea." I picked up one half of my burger and said, "Tell me more about Nessa."

I'd picked the right topic because he didn't press about the car thing. For the rest of the meal, Dad talked nonstop about his new girlfriend—a term that would take some getting used to. She sounded quirky and fun and perfect for him. I really hoped that was true, because if she ever hurt him, Ms. Broneicki would answer to me.

———

A SLEEPLESS NIGHT meant needing an extra cup of coffee to get moving on Monday morning. The forecast said clear skies so I walked down the hill to work, then half a block from the library, the drizzle started. Did I bring my umbrella? Of course not. I blamed the brain fog.

After dropping Dad at his house and staying long enough to accept the gift he brought me—a coffee mug featuring the Dallas skyline—I drove home lost in thought about the letter. Sharing with Dad was out of the question now. Maybe once he and this Nessa person had been together for a while, things would change, but until then, he didn't need Geraldine stepping back into his life.

Which left me with a conundrum. *Was I going to read it?*

Part of me said just get it over with. What if I was making a big deal out of nothing? But how could whatever she said not be a big deal? As the letter once again mocked me—this time from the coffee table—I paced my small living room, debating my next move. On one hand, I hadn't expected to hear from her ever again, and no matter what she said, I wanted nothing to do with her. I'd spent more of my life without a mother than with one and had turned out just fine. I had the best dad in the world, and that was the only parent I needed.

So why open it at all?

I paced again and played the other side of the argument. What if she was dying? What if she was homeless and needed money to get off the streets? No matter what I'd come up with during lunch on Saturday, I knew myself well enough to know that I'd never let anyone suffer if I could do something about it. Even the mother who didn't want me.

With a loud huff, I stomped in frustration before picking up the letter and marching to the tiny desk in the corner of the room. Before I could change my mind, I opened the bottom drawer, tossed in the envelope, and then slammed the drawer shut. And that was where it would stay. For now.

The stomping had initiated a tap on the ceiling below from Mr. Banks, and I yelled down an apology into the floor vent that had become our means of communication. Once that little trick had been discovered, I'd placed a thick rug over the vent, but it did come in handy at times.

"Good morning, Miriam," I said as I hung my damp sweater over the back of my chair. The air conditioning tended to make the library quite cold in the summers so I always carried a sweater with me. I wouldn't be wearing it today until it dried out.

"Good morning," she returned with an extra lilt in her tone. "How was your weekend?"

Had it really only been forty-eight hours since my meeting with Jeffrey had kicked off what could be called a series of unfortunate events? The *who did I tick off* trifecta, one might say.

"Eventful," I replied. "From that blush on your cheeks, I'm guessing yours was as well?"

Miriam giggled. "Our one-month anniversary dinner

stretched through the whole weekend. We both left my apartment at the same time this morning."

So things were definitely moving along. I could barely remember that high of new love, when the sun shone a little brighter and you felt as if you might never stop smiling. Becca was in that phase, and now so was Miriam. Lucky them.

"You're practically glowing," I said, genuinely happy for her. "You need to bring him in here soon so that we can meet him."

With a slight frown, she said, "He's going out of town on business but I want to introduce you soon."

"I can't wait." I logged into my computer and opened my email to find a message from Jeffrey.

Ms. Knox,

I will be meeting with the consultant next Friday. I'll need a detailed summary of each program on the list (attached) including costs and funding sources. Please have this to me no later than two days prior so I can review and request further information if necessary.

J. Chamberlain

"Did you just growl?" Miriam asked.

"Jeffrey sent me an email."

She rolled her chair over to mine. "What did he say?"

"He wants detailed summaries for every program we run, and he wants them by the middle of next week."

"As if you can just whip that up out of thin air."

I kept folders on every program, but they didn't

include this kind of detail, especially the programs that had been running for years. Some for decades.

"I have to do it. He's meeting with the consultant at the end of next week. The more information I arm him with, the better chance we have of saving our programs."

Miriam rolled back to her own station. "I'll help if I can, but I'm up to my eyeballs in the history event for next month."

We'd been gathering local stories since the start of the year, focusing on lesser-known characters who'd played key roles in the city's history but were rarely talked about. From Hugh J. Ward, a resident of Hazelwood who invented the game of Bingo, to Gus Greenlee, who'd dabbled in everything from running nightclubs to managing boxers and had even owned the Negro League's Pittsburgh Crawfords baseball team.

Miriam spearheaded the project and had done an amazing job curating an array of facts and figures from an assortment of sources. An exhibit would be on display for two weeks the following month and then carefully archived for anyone who wanted to learn more about the real people who had shaped the city.

"I'll take care of it," I said. "I just wish I could attend the meeting instead of Jeffrey. I don't trust him to stand up for the programs like he should."

"Morning, ladies," said Thomas as he stepped up to the counter. "How was your weekend?"

"Good," I said out of habit. "How was yours?"

"Nothing special since I was here for most of it. Miriam, I found some Pittsburgh Press articles from 1930 talking about that 805 thing you were researching. I put them in a folder on your desk."

"Oh, thank you." A second later, she made a squeaking sound that caused both Thomas and I to look her way. Miriam covered her mouth, her eyes shifting from Thomas to me and back. "Could you grab me some printer paper from downstairs?" she said to him.

"Sure." He looked confused but marched off toward the stairs.

Once he was gone, she rolled my way. "I am the worst friend ever. How could I forget to ask how it went with Fletcher and his girlfriend? Was it hard? Is she pretty?" Holding a hand up palm out, she shook her head. "Forget I asked that. It's petty and sexist. Are you okay?"

I appreciated her concern, though I found it almost funny that when I'd left work on Friday, Fletcher's new relationship had been my only concern. Now Fletcher was the least of my worries.

CHAPTER SEVEN

"I'M FINE. FIONA IS NICE. AND GORGEOUS. AND A really good player." Jaw tight, I added, "Fletcher is another story."

Miriam lowered her voice to a conspiratorial whisper. "What did he do?"

I spun to face her and crossed my arms as I summarized. "First, he sent a text asking if I wanted a ride to practice."

"As if."

"Exactly. Then he caught me at the start of practice and said he was glad that I decided to play. As if I might be too brokenhearted to play on the team I've been fighting to join since before I met him."

Miriam mirrored my pose. "He makes me so mad. I wish you didn't have to deal with him."

I hadn't mentioned Ryan at lunch on Saturday, but

then I'd been too distracted by the letter. Today, I needed to vent about that situation as well.

"There's a new guy on the team. He just moved to the city earlier in the year and we seemed to hit it off."

Her anger fled as she sat up straighter. "Oh, this is good. What's his name? Did you get his number?"

She was about to get angry all over again. "I didn't get that far thanks to Fletcher. He said something to Ryan during a water break and from then on he barely looked my way."

"Wait, Ryan is the new guy?"

"Yes."

"And Fletcher said something to make him stop talking to you?"

I didn't know that for sure. "He could have said anything, but why else would this guy suddenly start treating me like I was off-limits?"

"You are very much on-*limits*," Miriam paused. "In-limits? Whatever it is, you're available and this guy needs to know that."

"Right? I'm going to see what happens at practice tonight before I decide whether or not to say something. I mean, I don't know much about the new guy. He could be taken or just not interested, but if Fletcher *is* the reason for the abrupt change of attitude, I want to know."

Expression softening, she tapped me on the leg. "I like this feistiness. You're getting some of your old spark back."

I'd never thought of myself as having any sort of spark. "I don't know about that."

"I do. And I like it."

"Here's the paper," Thomas said, returning with a ream in hand.

Miriam took the offering. "Thank you, sir." Opening her desk drawer, she dropped it in on top of the full ream she already had.

"Why did you send me down for that if you already had some?" he asked.

Flashing her brightest, most innocent smile, she said, "A girl can never have too much paper."

Thomas had worked with women long enough to know when to stop asking questions. "Right. I'm going to check the drop box for returns while you two keep talking about whatever it is you don't want me to hear."

As our coworker walked away, Miriam said, "He's smarter than he looks."

"He has two master's degrees and three sisters," I reminded her.

"Good point. Too bad the two of you dating isn't an option."

"I think Stephanie would frown on that." Thomas and his wife had been together for at least four years now. "Besides, I wouldn't want to date a coworker."

Finally firing up her computer, Miriam nodded. "That's fair. But team members don't count in that, right?"

I couldn't eliminate all possibilities. "Team members do not count as coworkers."

With a sly smile, she said, "Good. I can't wait to come to your first game and see this new man for myself. I might give Fletcher a piece of my mind as well."

"That will not be happening." Though it was tempting to sic Miriam on him. That would be even more satisfying than watching Jacob scare the heck out of him.

"You're no fun."

———

WITH ONLY TWO weeks before the season started, we had practice every other day going forward. I made sure not to be late this time.

"Hey, lady. You want to warm up?" Roxanne asked as I dropped my bag near the bench.

"Sure."

I withdrew my glove from the bag after tossing in my keys and then jogged into left field not far behind her. A quick scan of the field showed that Ryan had yet to arrive. I had no idea if he'd talk to me again, or if he'd go back to acting as if we never met.

Part of me said this weird preoccupation with a man I barely knew was childish and probably pointless. He'd been kind. So were a lot of people. But his attitude had taken such an abrupt turn after Fletcher spoke to him, I couldn't help but wonder. Was he that easily put off, or had everything before that been my imagination?

The coach called us in and I still hadn't seen Ryan, so I assumed someone else would be playing shortstop today.

"As you all know, we have less than two weeks before our first game," Coach Barry said. "Yinz know how to play, but we need to work on how to play *together*. I'm going to leave the positions just like we had them on Friday, so hit the field and we'll get started."

I opened my mouth to ask who would play shortstop, but before I could speak up, Ryan walked past me onto the field. Where the heck did he come from?

"Hey!" I said, catching up to him. "When did you get here?"

"I had a late meeting, so I just made it when everyone was coming in." He didn't say more or look happy to chat.

"Did I do something on Friday?"

Punching the center of his glove, Ryan said, "Look, I don't want to get in the middle of anything."

"Here we go!" yelled the coach seconds before I heard the ball hit the bat. Spinning, I turned in time to duck as Theresa made her throw from third to first base. "You're next, Ryan."

Fuming, I trotted into position and waited my turn. When the ball came my way, I scooped it up and threw a line drive straight at Fletcher's head. Unfortunately, his reflexes were good and he caught the ball in his glove instead of in his big mouth.

"What was that for?" he said before tossing the ball back to home plate.

I ignored him and got back into position. Every throw I made to first for the next fifteen minutes was an attempt to plant the ball in his forehead. While practicing the double play, I sailed one from the second base bag that he wasn't fast enough for. The ball pinged off his shoulder and I experienced a moment of deep satisfaction.

"You've got to catch that," Coach Barry said to Fletcher, and I turned to face the outfield to hide my grin.

I wasn't normally a violent person, and it wasn't as if I had anything with Ryan that my ex could ruin, but Fletcher had definitely interfered somehow, which set my teeth on edge. We were no longer together because of him. I'd thought he was the one. In fact, I had stupidly assumed that he was going to propose the night he took me to a fancy restaurant on Mount Washington just to *break up with me*. Also, his new girlfriend was *on the team*, for heaven's sake. Did she know that he was telling guys not to talk to me? She probably wouldn't appreciate him interfering in my life any more than I did.

"What is wrong with you?" Fletcher growled in my ear as we headed off the field for our first break.

"It isn't my fault you can't catch the ball," I replied without sparing him a glance.

"You're trying to take my head off."

Stopping, I turned with narrowed eyes. "If I really wanted to hurt you, I'd have planted that ball between your eyes by now and you know I could do it."

"You're kicking butt today, Megan," said Fiona as she came up behind us. "Nice arm."

"Thank you," I said, flashing Fletcher a screw-you smile. "Say, Fiona, how long have you and Fletcher been together?"

I asked the question loud enough for all to hear and wasn't surprised to see Ryan look our way with a confused gaze.

"It'll be four months next week," she replied. "If I keep him that long." The chuckle that followed those words revealed quite a bit about their relationship. She was kidding, but there was an underlying thread of truth, too.

"You two are dating?" Ryan asked her.

"Yeah," she said. "You didn't know?"

Brown eyes narrowed on Fletcher. "No, I thought—"

"Now everyone knows," Fletcher cut in. "Babe, let me get you some water." He dragged Fiona to the cooler and elbowed past two people to grab a paper cup.

I took a seat on the bench and Ryan dropped down next to me. "I didn't—" he started, but I would not let him apologize for something that wasn't his fault.

"Fletcher and I dated for three years, but we broke up eight months ago. I don't know why he'd make you think otherwise."

"I can think of one reason," he replied.

Shaking my head, I watched my ex hand his new girl-friend a cup of water. "We haven't even spoken since we broke up. Not until last Friday, anyway. Trust me, there's nothing there."

We sat in silence after that, but a good silence. The kind where you know a hurdle just got moved out of the way, and you get to decide if you want to move on past it.

"We're good then?" he asked.

I wasn't completely sure what that meant, but I nodded. "I'm good if you are."

"Yeah. All good."

Barely breathing, I waited for him to say more, but the silence continued until Coach called us back to the field. There were a few smiles exchanged as we once again worked in sync at second base, but nothing beyond that. Maybe he was shy. I'd gone out of my way to make sure he knew about Fletcher and Fiona, so at least now he knew I was available.

As practice came to an end, we walked off the field together and I tried to muster up the courage to ask him something. Anything. Was he going to the bar with everyone else? Was he free this weekend? Did he like short brunettes who owned too many books?

"Who all is coming to the bar?" Dalton asked, and as players said yes or no, I glanced over to Ryan.

"Are you going?" I asked.

"Are you?" he said.

I couldn't tell if his tone was hopeful or just curious. "I can go for a little while."

Ryan nodded as his full lips turned up in a heart stopping grin. "Then I'll see you there."

———

THE OUTSIDE of Alexion's wasn't much to look at. A rectangular boxlike building, the two-story structure consisted of a combination of concrete blocks, red bricks, and beige siding around most of the upper story. It was like a Lego build pieced together with whatever spare bricks the person could find. The inside was much nicer, but still your standard Pittsburgh bar. Lots of dark wood. A sports mural on the back wall. Traditional bar decor and sturdy wooden tables. The moment you entered you could feel the history of the place, and the smells coming from the kitchen made your mouth water.

A seemingly endless list of craft brews was listed on the chalkboard over the bar, and I watched a waitress walk by with a loaded tray of sandwiches roughly the size of my head. This was a place for hearty meals, draft beers, and neighborhood camaraderie. A place that screamed *welcome to the Burgh.*

"We've got a bunch of tables in the back," Jeremy said when he spotted me scanning the room. He was at the end of the bar, presumably putting in an order. "What can I get you?"

"I'll take an Angry Orchard Rosé." I wasn't a huge beer drinker, but the ciders I could do.

"You got it."

I headed for the tables Jeremy mentioned as he called out my order to the bartender. When I reached the group, I didn't see Ryan, but Fletcher was animatedly telling a story at the far end of the tables. Fiona was nowhere in sight, so I assumed maybe she'd skipped again.

There were two empty chairs beside Theresa so I took the one next to her and hoped that Ryan would take the other. Unfortunately, Jeremy sat down instead after passing around a collection of drinks. The Angry Orchard landed in front of me at the same time a waitress set down a paper basket of celery with ranch dressing.

"You've got one hell of an arm," Jeremy said. I waited for him to add "for a girl" but he ended the sentence there.

"Thanks."

"That was smart what you did at practice."

Unsure what he meant, I asked, "What was smart?"

"Pointing out that Fletcher and Fiona are a thing. Some of us know the history between you two. We wondered if there might be some drama that would get in the way of the season. That told us it's all cool."

As I processed this information, Theresa said, "I told yinz guys that Megan wasn't the drama type."

I couldn't decide whether to be annoyed that they'd

been talking behind my back or grateful that someone had stuck up for me.

"You never know," Jeremy said before turning his attention to Priscilla on his other side.

Still speechless, I stared at my drink as Theresa said, "Ignore him. The guys don't get it, but us girls know what Fletcher is like."

"What he's like?" I repeated. For the three years I was with Fletcher, I never heard anyone say a bad word about him.

She glanced down the table at Fletcher and dropped her voice. "He's full of shit ninety percent of the time."

That would have been nice to know three years ago. "What does that have to do with what Jeremy said?"

"Fletcher has been telling people that you're trying to get him back." Theresa scoffed. "I never believed it."

The man literally dumped me and then ignored me for eight months. He also had a beautiful girlfriend. Why tell such a lie?

"From the time I moved out up until last Friday, I never even spoke to him. Why would he tell people that?"

"Because he's needy," she replied. "He's probably been asked a couple hundred times where you are and why you guys broke up. Personally, I don't blame you for dumpin' his ass."

"*I* dumped *him*?"

"Didn't you?"

I clearly needed to straighten a few things out. "No, I

didn't. That was Fletcher's decision. And I haven't made any effort to get back together with him. Considering he has Fiona now, I don't see the point of him saying that. I mean, he's moved on."

"Has he?" she said with an arched brow.

This was ridiculous. "Him dating Fiona makes me believe so, yeah."

"Then why did he tell Ryan to stay away from you?"

I slapped my hand on the table. "That's what he told him?"

Theresa picked up her beer. "That's what I heard from third base."

The nerve of this man. Whether anything happened between me and Ryan, Fletcher had no business saying something like that to anyone. *He didn't want me.*

"Fletcher and I need to have a talk." Shoving my chair back, I marched to the end of the table. "I need a word with you," I said, interrupting his conversation.

Looking surprised and exceedingly uncomfortable, he said, "Sure. What do you need?"

"Outside." I took off for the entrance without looking back, certain that he'd follow. As I pushed the door open, someone pulled from the other side and sent me flying into a solid chest.

"Hey," Ryan said, righting me before I could fall to my knees. "Are you going somewhere?"

"I've got her," Fletcher said, taking my hand and dragging me into the parking lot.

"I'll be right back," I yelled before jerking my hand away. The insufferable man stopped beside his car as I said, "What is wrong with you?"

"You're the one who just made a scene."

He would not turn this on me. "*You're* the one telling people I'm trying to get you back. Why would you lie like that?"

His eyes cut to the passing cars. "I never said that."

"And I suppose you didn't tell Ryan to leave me alone either?"

"You don't even know him."

"Neither do you." Trying to get a handle on my temper, I paced away from him.

"I didn't like the way he was looking at you," Fletcher said.

Charging back again, I pointed out the obvious. "*You* don't get to decide how men look at me. You broke up with me, remember?" He remained silent and I tried to understand what this was all about. "Have you changed your mind? Is that what's going on here? And if so, what about Fiona?"

Fletcher slammed his hands into the pockets of his sweatpants before leaning on his car door. "Fiona has nothing to do with this."

"Yes, she does. She's your girlfriend, or have you forgotten about that?"

"I'm sorry, okay. Is that what you want to hear?"

This had been the one rift between us when we were

dating. Fletcher hated to argue. He'd say whatever he had to in order to end a fight and then pretend that nothing happened. This meant nothing got resolved because he'd rather sweep things under the rug than actually deal with them.

"Not if you don't mean it. Just stay out of my life, Fletcher, and I'll stay out of yours."

I turned to walk away and he said, "I never asked for that. I thought we could stay friends."

Did he suffer from short-term memory loss?

"Until that text last Friday, I haven't heard a word from you, so excuse me if I didn't get the *stay friends* memo." Poking him in the chest, I added, "And if this is your idea of being my friend, I'm not interested."

"I wanted to give you your space," he said. "You know, to get over things."

Was I upset when we broke up? Of course I was. Did I cry my eyes out for months missing him? No, I did not. Being bitter about the reason he broke up with me did not mean that I was still in love with him.

I pinched the bridge of my nose as I tried to figure out how to make myself clear.

"Look, we had some good times. A lot of them. But you said yourself that we're too different. Now you've found someone else, a woman with whom I assume you share more in common than you did with me, and I'm moving on as well. Whether that happens with Ryan or someone else is none of your business."

I turned again to leave, but he had one more question. "What about being friends?"

I stopped but didn't turn around. Letting out a long sigh, I said, "We're teammates, Fletcher. Let's leave it at that."

CHAPTER EIGHT

FLETCHER WAS RIGHT ABOUT ONE THING. I *HAD* CAUSED A scene, and I regretted it the moment I rejoined the group when a hush fell over the tables. Being the center of attention had never appealed to me, but I had to do something to break the silence.

"Anyone up for a game of darts?" I asked.

"Heck, yeah," Dalton said, rising from his chair.

Theresa rose as well. "I'll play. Come on, Jeremy. Let's kick their butts."

I looked around to find Ryan, hoping he might play as well, but he wasn't sitting with the others.

"Where's Ryan?" I asked Theresa.

With a shrug, she plucked the darts out of the pock-marked board. "He said something about having to get home to Wendy."

My brain skidded to a stop. "Wendy?"

"Yeah. Probably his girlfriend. No way a guy that cute is single."

Hopes crushed, I nodded. "Right."

She handed me the three blue darts. "He was flirting with you pretty hard, though, so maybe it's his sister or something."

Or maybe I'd completely misread the situation and was about to make a fool of myself. I'd only met the guy twice now so it wasn't as if I was invested, but I had hoped…

"Are you as good at darts as you are at softball?" Dalton asked while dangling an arm around my shoulders.

The smell of sweat smacked me in the nose and I tried not to breathe too deeply. "Are you?" I asked.

He winked. "I'm good at a lot of things."

Flirting wasn't my forte, and neither was recognizing when I was being flirted with. However, even I recognized such a blatant come-on. Dipping out from beneath his arm, I put some distance between us. "I'm only interested in your dart skills, but good to know."

Undeterred, the outfielder grinned with confidence. "We can start there."

Well aware of his playboy reputation, I ignored the comment. He was pretty and would probably show any girl a good time, but that was the problem. For Dalton, any girl would do, and I wasn't interested in becoming one more name on his score sheet.

"You must have ripped Fletcher a new one," Theresa said in a low whisper as Jeremy took his turn.

"We just cleared a few things up," I said.

She nudged me with her elbow and pointed toward the group with her dart. "He hasn't said a word since he came back in. I've never seen the man so quiet."

He did look a bit pathetic, and I tried not to feel guilty. This was his fault, after all. I didn't break up with him. And I wasn't the one interfering in his life. In fact, I was trying to stay *out* of his life. At any time over the last eight months, Fletcher could have called or sent an email. He could have come into the library or stopped by my house. I wasn't hiding, and I hadn't blocked him in any way.

Yet, he'd done none of those things.

"How well do you know Fiona?" I asked her.

"Not much, but I know she's too good for his ass."

Dalton finished his turn, scoring enough points to take us into the lead, and Theresa stepped up to go.

"What are you doing this weekend?" Dalton asked, leaning an arm on the cocktail table against the wall.

Where did this sudden interest come from? Was I putting out a pheromone I wasn't aware of? Because guys like Dalton typically didn't take an interest in me. I was the short, quiet one who was good for an extra base hit. Dalton's targets were more the party girls looking for a good time. There was nothing wrong with that, but it just wasn't me.

"I'm not sure," I said, too stunned to come up with a lie. "I might be working."

Not a lie, necessarily. I did have that programs summary to do for Jeffrey.

"You're up, Megan," said Jeremy. "Let's see what you've got."

Happy for the out, I stepped up to the line and took my turn. I'd played on a darts team back in college and still had the muscle memory to hit every number I aimed for. Though we weren't on the same team, Theresa offered a high five while the guys stared with gaping jaws.

"What the hell?" Jeremy said.

"That's my partner," Dalton replied with a grin.

Impressing him had not been my intention, but I would never tank a game on purpose, even to get out of an awkward situation. Damn my competitive nature. Though he stood a little too close every chance he got, my teammate didn't pursue the weekend question through the rest of the game, and once we won—by a blowout, of course—I turned my darts over to Priscilla and said my goodbyes.

Fletcher and I didn't speak again, and when Dalton offered to walk me to my car, I firmly but nicely turned him down. To my relief, he took the rejection well, and I was in my car minutes later. On the drive home, my brain kept going back to the Wendy thing. How could I have been so far off? Better to find out now than later, but still.

That glimmer of hope had been the one positive in a series of *what the hells*.

If asked a week ago, I'd have said I wished my life wasn't so boring. After the last four days, boring sounded really flippin' good.

———

NOT COUNTING the looming stress of Jeffrey and our endangered programs, work was still my safe haven. My calm in whatever storm might be brewing in my life. Though I couldn't remember a time when I didn't love books, I once realized that I also felt protective of them. I doubt I would have survived my mother's abrupt departure without the ability to escape from my fear and guilt and loneliness into other worlds. Secret gardens and magical wardrobes and, of course, the wizarding world that had bewitched a generation.

Books were there when the birthday cards stopped coming. When graduations passed without her there. Even as recently as when Fletcher said he didn't want me anymore. I owed my sanity and my imagination to books, and being a librarian was my way of paying them back.

But the job came with one more benefit—meeting people who loved books as much as I did.

"I can't believe you have this," said Ruby, gently trailing a hand over the cover of a fifty-year-old copy of *Charlotte's Web*. "This is my most favorite-est story."

Her reverence for the book made my heart swell. "Why do you like that one so much?" I asked her. I had my reasons for loving Charlotte, but I wanted to know Ruby's reasons.

"Because I'm Wilbur," she said, taking me by surprise.

"You're Wilbur?"

Ruby nodded. "He needed a mom and Charlotte took care of him. Then he lost her." Kicking her feet back and forth beneath her chair, she kept her eyes on the weathered cover. "My mom took really good care of me, and then I lost her."

I hadn't expected to cry at work today. "You miss her a lot, huh?"

Blue eyes rose to mine. "Do you miss your mom?"

When she'd first started coming to the library, Ruby had been quiet and standoffish. Once I learned her story, I shared my own to let her know she wasn't alone in not having a mother. Mine wasn't killed in an accident, but she was out of my life just the same.

This was not an easy question to answer. After some consideration, I said, "I miss having a mom, yes."

I couldn't lie and say I missed my mother specifically. I didn't even know her, really. No more than a seven-year-old could have. But most of my memories weren't good. I assumed that Ruby didn't have many memories of her mother either. She'd only been a toddler at the time of the accident.

"Do you like your dad?" she asked.

"I love my dad," I replied without hesitation. "He's my favorite person in the whole world. Do you like your dad?"

Russell Adams seemed like a good man, but I hadn't been around him much since Ruby's aunt, her father's younger sister, accompanied the child to the library most of the time.

"Papa is okay," she replied without much enthusiasm. "He works a lot but he always gets home in time to tuck me in."

"Does he read to you?" I asked.

"Sometimes." As if wanting to change the subject, Ruby said, "You're in this book, too."

I could see myself as Fern. A little girl passionate to save a little pig.

"Who do you see me as?" I asked, assuming I knew the answer.

Ruby scooted to the edge of her chair. "You're Charlotte."

Confused, I asked, "How so?"

"You're always telling us that we're special, and you read to us, and you teach us things. You're like a mom."

Now I really was going to cry. I wanted children but had long feared that my unconventional upbringing had left me ill-equipped to be a mother. Not that Dad hadn't been a wonderful parent, but moms were different. Moms had special powers, and if those were passed down or learned, then I would never have them.

Chest tight with gratitude, I said, "I've never pictured myself as a spider, but that comparison makes me happy."

With a nod, she hopped off her chair. "You should. I need to use the little girls' room."

The abrupt change of topic made me smile. "Just leave the book on your chair," I said and watched her shuffle off toward the stairs. On my way back to the front desk, I passed Cassie, her nose deep in an old newspaper. "Have you found something interesting?" I asked.

She glanced up, eyes blinking as if she'd been looking at the tiny print for too long.

"Interesting, yes. Helpful, no."

I sat down across the table from her. "What exactly *are* you looking for?"

Cassie closed the newspaper, careful not to tear it. "Anything that will tell me about my mom's side of the family."

I didn't want to assume, so I said, "Can you not ask your mom?"

"I have." Her lips fell into a flat line. "She says I don't need to go digging through the past."

Odd, but I supposed every family had their secrets. Some that probably should stay buried.

"She must have her reasons. What if you find something you don't want to know?"

"Learning anything would be better than the big blank space that's there now." Crossing her arms, she leaned back in her chair. "My mom and I don't get along, but she's the only parent I've ever known, and I'm tired of not having a history."

"You don't have to answer this, but you never knew your dad?"

Cassie shook her head. "He died when Luke and I were still babies."

"Luke is your brother?"

"My twin," she said with a nod. "Mom moved us away from his family and they didn't make an effort to keep in touch, but I do know a little about them. That isn't the case for Mom's side. I did the DNA thing, but nothing came up that would give me any leads."

I considered doing that once, but never got around to it. "I'm sorry that you aren't finding any answers."

"Me, too." She sighed. "I was hoping I'd discover a whole family, and then there'd be reunions and big holiday gatherings. Some kind of medical history would be nice, too."

Funny I hadn't thought about those things. Geraldine had been an only child plus a late in life baby so her parents had both passed when I was too young to know them. Dad had a couple sisters so we did the occasional holiday dinner. One of my cousins had kids and I always took books for them, but we hadn't gotten together in quite a while. Geraldine had been healthy during the seven years she'd been with us, but I wondered if she'd had any medical conditions since then. Maybe that's what was in the letter.

Then again, if she hadn't cared enough to stay in my life, I couldn't imagine she'd take the time to warn me of an impending fatal disease.

"Do you know anything about her life here in Pittsburgh?" I asked.

"Zilch," Cassie replied.

I tried to think of ways to help. "If you know her date of birth, you might try looking for a birth certificate."

"Already did that and got nothing. It's as if she never existed before moving to California."

Whatever this woman wanted to hide must have been huge. Like she'd killed a man, or maybe she'd been involved with some mafia type and knew too much. Pittsburgh had been home to a slew of organized crime families throughout the twentieth century, and some were still wielding power as recently as the last decade.

"That *is* odd. Whatever she isn't telling you must be a big deal."

With a roll of her eyes, Cassie said, "She just likes to be mysterious. The woman has been a bookkeeper for a dental office since I was a kid. That doesn't exactly scream wild and crazy past."

Unless she learned how to keep books through a nefarious enterprise.

I rose to my feet. "Local history is Miriam's area so she might be more help than I am."

"We spent an hour together the other day and still found nothing, but I'm not ready to give up yet." Cassie opened the newspaper once more. "I'm determined to find answers."

"Good luck."

"Thanks," she said. "I could use some."

I did a quick check on Ruby, who was back and happily reading about Wilbur and Charlotte, then returned to my desk, trying to recall the details I knew about Geraldine's life before having me. She and Dad had gone to the same high school, and I'd found her in his old yearbook. From what I could gather, she'd been pretty, popular, and involved in everything. Cheerleading. Drama club. Student council. Even the yearbook committee, which probably explained why her picture showed up every few pages.

Geraldine had liked attention. I'd once wished to be more like her. To be bold and outgoing. But I would never want to be a mother like her. My children, should I ever be lucky enough to have some, would never experience what I did.

CHAPTER NINE

I WAS LESS STRESSED GOING INTO THE NEXT PRACTICE than I'd been before the first two. There was no more trepidation about Fletcher. He knew where I stood, and thinking of him with someone else didn't make my stomach roll like it did last week. Though I'd been hopeful about Ryan, finding out he had a Wendy at home, which I doubted was a sister or whatever Theresa had suggested, snapped some common sense into me.

He was a stranger who had been nice to me for fewer than thirty minutes. Beyond that, I knew nothing about him. He could hate romantic comedies. Or like yacht rock. Or eat pineapple on his pizza.

The dealbreaker possibilities were endless.

What if he didn't like books or cats or Pokémon plushies? I owned a great deal of two of these items, and I did not have a cat. Fletcher had hated my plushie collection, so I'd been forced to put them all in totes that had collected dust in his garage. No longer did I have to hide them away, and I'd vowed never again to put a man above my Pokémon.

I arrived extra early today, and to my surprise, Fiona asked to warm up with me. Fletcher had yet to show, and I had no reason to turn her down so I agreed. Her arm really was impressive. She stung my hand a couple of times, but I could tell she wasn't doing it on purpose. That was just how the threw. Like a shot coming at you. At one point, the ball lifted in the air like a curveball catching a current and I couldn't help but envy her talent.

She was the perfect argument for why there should be more opportunities for women's softball beyond college. There technically was a professional league, but most people had never heard of it, and it wasn't even close to the level of professional baseball. The lack of opportunities in this sport was so frustrating.

The good thing about warming up with Fiona was that I had to pay attention. Stealing glances to see the arriving teammates could cost me my nose. Which was why I didn't see Ryan until the coach had called us all to the bench. Without much preamble, we took to the field, filling the same positions from the previous practices, and the men to my left and right both acted as if I wasn't there.

I understood Fletcher's behavior. I didn't think I'd been unnecessarily mean the other night, but I hadn't been my typical doormat self either. Whatever issue he had with his decision to break up with me was his to deal with. There had been plenty of moments over the last eight months when I'd wanted to hear from him, but that feeling had passed.

Ryan's attitude was more confusing. He now knew there was nothing between me and Fletcher, and if anything, I should have been the one annoyed, since he clearly had someone waiting at home.

The first half of practice progressed as usual, and we took a water break before switching to batting practice. I waited my turn, then filled my cup and took a seat on the bench. Ryan did the same but remained standing several feet away. Everyone took their turn, and after another twenty minutes of practicing several defensive plays, Coach Barry gathered us at the bench once again.

"As you all know, our first game is a week from today. I considered adding another practice over the weekend, but we don't need it. We'll be here next Monday and Wednesday, and at that point, I'll have your shirts to hand out. Don't do anything stupid in the next week. I don't want to start the season having to find coverage for injured players. Any questions?"

No one spoke.

"Good. Then be back here at six on Monday."

The usual call for the bar came up, and I opted out. Dalton had already winked at me twice; Fletcher was clearly still sulking, and Alexion's would be much more packed on a Friday than they'd been on Wednesday night. There was a hot bath, green tea face mask, and the latest Kristin Hannah book waiting for me at home.

"Can I talk to you a second?" Ryan said, surprising me as I reached my car.

"Sure," I replied, telling myself not to read anything into this. "What do you need?"

He looked around as if to make sure he wouldn't be overheard. "Is there anything between you and Fletcher or not?"

Annoyed, I said, "Not."

"Then what was that at the bar?"

I sighed, debating how to answer. Technically, this was none of his business, but since Fletcher had been spreading one very big lie, it was probably best to tell him the truth. "I found out that he was telling people I want him back, which I don't. I took him outside to clear that up."

"It looked more like he took *you* outside."

Not liking that implication, I rose to my full five foot two inches and said, "I ran into you because I reached the door first. Because I told him I needed to talk to him outside and he was following me. Now I have a question for you. Why are you so worried about me and Fletcher when you have Wendy at home?"

The man had the nerve to smile. "Wendy is my dog."

He sure knew how to take the wind out of a girl's sails. "Your dog?" The nod paired with a smirk said I'd just outed myself as a jealous woman. Embarrassment made my cheeks hot. "I didn't know you had a dog."

"And I didn't know that you were done with Fletcher." Lifting his ball cap, he ran a hand through his thick brown hair. "How about we try this from the beginning?" Dropping the cap back into place, he extended a hand. "I'm Ryan Stallings. Nice to meet you."

He could be really charming when he wanted to be. "I'm Megan Knox," I said, accepting the handshake.

"I know we just met," he said, struggling to control his grin, "but would you like to have dinner with me?"

My heart fell to my knees as I tried to keep up the pretense. Gosh, he was beautiful when he smiled. "I don't even know you," I pointed out, attempting to flip my hair over my shoulder and forgetting it was up in a ponytail.

Ryan snorted but recovered quickly. "There's only one way to fix that. What do you say?"

Since I was so bad at it, I dropped the act. "You mean tonight?"

"I was thinking more like tomorrow. Something nicer than sweaty T-shirts and ball caps."

As if resurrected, my heart shot right back into my chest and started beating double time. "I'd like that."

"Good." He leaned forward and I thought he might kiss me, but instead he opened the hatch on my car and held it open. "We can't have you hit your head again."

The giggle that escaped my lips made me sound like a middle schooler. "Thank you." I tossed my bag inside and stepped away so he could let the hatch close. "If you give me your phone, I'll put in my number."

He did as asked, and I hit save a few seconds later. Once I handed it back, he touched the screen a few times, and then my phone dinged.

"That's me," he said. "Seven tomorrow? You can text me your address."

Mesmerized by the twinkle in his eye, all I could do was nod in approval.

Backing away, he said, "See you tomorrow, Megan."

My name had never sounded so sexy before. "See you, Ryan."

He took several more steps before turning around to walk to his car. I watched him go to see what he drove and was relieved when he climbed into a very practical white Chevy Cruze.

With a sigh, I came to my senses and caught sight of Fletcher farther down the parking lot. He was standing with his door open, watching me over the roof of his car. Once we made eye contact, he shook his head and climbed in. The red Charger peeled out of the parking lot seconds later.

If he expected me to feel guilty about going out with another man, then he would be highly disappointed. He'd made his decision and hadn't even given me a choice. There'd been no discussion. Just we're through *and* he'd made me feel like it was my fault. Now I was moving on, just as he had with Fiona. If he didn't like it, that was his problem, not mine.

Shoving my ex out of my head, I replayed the last two minutes and could not stop smiling. Did that really happen? Wait. I was going on a date. In twenty-four hours. Holy crap.

I was going on a date.

SOMETIME IN THE year after we all graduated college, my friends and I established group chats. These happened when one person sent out an SOS of sorts, and the others dropped whatever they were doing to answer the call. Back then, we had to do them in person, but thanks to modern technology, we could all be scattered yet still present and ready to listen.

Being asked on a date didn't necessarily qualify as an SOS situation, but I was invoking the chat anyway, because I had no idea what to wear or what to say and this called for reinforcements.

"What's going on?" Becca said as she popped into the video chat. She was sitting on her couch with her laptop and I could see her cat Milo peering over her shoulder.

"We're waiting for Lindsey," Josie said with an eye roll. "She's at some parent-teacher thing but said she'll be on in a few."

"Is this about that letter from your mom?" Donna asked.

"Not the letter." I was slouched against my headboard with my knees up at nose level.

"No one is sick or hurt?" Josie asked. "Pops is okay?"

The girls all loved Dad, as everyone did. "Dad is good. In fact, he's seeing someone."

Donna dropped her phone as Becca said, "Daddy Knox has a girlfriend?"

"Holy shit," Donna said. "You've got to warn a girl before dropping a bomb like that."

"Sorry." I slouched down even deeper. "He just told me about her on Sunday. Her name is Nessa, and I'm hoping to meet her soon."

"I'm here," Lindsey cut in as another box popped up. There was no one in the frame.

"Are you in your car?" Becca asked as we all squinted at our screens.

An engine roared to life. "I'm driving home and you all are on the passenger seat. What's going on?"

I pulled the collar of my T-shirt up over my chin. "I have a date," I mumbled.

"You what?" Josie said.

I sat up a bit. "I have a date tomorrow."

"With who?" Becca asked.

"A guy on my softball team."

"Tell me you are not going back out with Fletcher,"

Donna snapped, looking ready to come through the phone and beat some sense into me.

"Not Fletcher. His name is Ryan."

"You called a chat because you have a date?" Lindsey chimed in. "Woman, that is not an emergency."

"It is when you haven't been on a first date in nearly four years." Pulling a Squirtle plushie into my lap, I added, "I don't know what to wear, or where we're even going. He just said something nicer than sweaty T-shirts and ball caps."

Donna snorted. "That could be anywhere."

"Are you letting him pick you up?" Josie asked, ever the protective one of the group. "Are you sure you want him to know where you live? How well do you know him?"

"Not well," I answered honestly. "I just met him at the first practice last week."

"Did you already give him your address?"

"Watch where you're going, jackass!" yelled Lindsey. We were used to her road-raging ways and ignored her.

"Yes, I did. Josie, he's a nice guy, not an ax murderer."

Throwing her hands in the air, she rolled her eyes. "That you know of."

"There's no reason to assume the worst," Becca pointed out, ever the peacekeeper. "What does he do for a living, Meg?"

"He works in finance."

Donna cackled. "We know how dangerous those people are."

The rest of us laughed, but Josie wasn't amused. "Chuckle all you want, but this is a serious matter." Pointing at her computer screen, she added, "Let us know where he takes you, and check in throughout the evening. If I don't hear from you every hour, I'm coming to find you."

"Aren't you playing cards tomorrow night?" Donna asked.

Josie was as competitive as I was, but athletics weren't her thing. She preferred tabletop games. If cards were involved, all the better.

"I'll dip out for Megan if I have to," she replied.

"Me, too," said Lindsey. "Not that I have anything to dip out of tomorrow night, but I'll drive the getaway car." That led to groans from the rest of us. "I'm a good driver, damn it." Before we could respond, a car horn blared and she shouted, "I had my blinker on, dumbass!"

"Can we maybe let Lindsey go?" asked Becca. "Before she kills herself or someone else? I think the rest of us can handle this issue."

"I'm not going to kill anyone."

"Maybe not," said Donna, "but I'm getting car sick watching that air freshener on your mirror sway back and forth."

The frame went black as she flipped the phone.

"There. Now you can't see it. Come on, guys. I'll just listen."

"You're fine, Lindsey." I hopped off my bed. "So the first problem. What do I wear?" Crossing to my closet, I dragged the doors open and flipped the camera on my phone so they could see my wardrobe. "Dress? Jeans? What?"

"I vote jeans," Donna said.

Josie nodded. "I agree."

"That does sound like your best bet. Unless he seems like a more formal guy." Becca rubbed Milo's head absently. "What's he look like anyway? You haven't told us anything about him."

I dropped back onto the bed. "He's maybe five foot nine. Brown eyes with ridiculously long lashes. Wavy brown hair a tad on the long side." I fell onto my back and pictured his face in my mind. "He has a great smile. The kind where one side of his mouth curls up before the other side, and his face slowly gets brighter as the smile grows. Then he looks at you like that and you forget how to breathe." Silence followed and I realized what I'd said. Clearing my throat, I sat back up. "I mean. He's a cute guy."

"Well shit," Donna said. "Does he have a brother?"

"You're such a goner," Josie teased. "I forgot you've always fallen way faster than the rest of us."

That didn't sound right. "Since when?"

"You moved in with Fletcher after how long?" she asked.

"Three weeks," Becca answered for me.

"That was only because my lease was up, and his roommate was moving out." I scooted back up to my headboard. "Neither of us could afford to live alone back then."

"So he moved you in to pay half the bills," Donna said. "How romantic."

This was not supposed to be a review of my past mistakes.

"So I'm wearing jeans tomorrow, and I'll let you guys know where we're going. I think we're done here."

"Seriously," Donna said, sobering. "Be careful. It doesn't sound like you know much about this guy beyond that swoony smile of his. Remember, the one commonality among serial killers is that no one ever guessed they were serial killers."

A disturbing thought. "He has a dog named Wendy. I can't imagine a serial killer having a dog named Wendy."

"Maybe he gets rid of the bodies by feeding them to the dog," Lindsey suggested.

"Ew. You *have* to stop watching the ID channel." To me, Becca said, "Have a good time tomorrow, but definitely let us know the location." As if jumping on the killer theory bandwagon, she added, "Just in case."

This was getting out of hand. "Guys, I'll be fine. I'll be nervous and probably make a fool of myself, but I will not be killed. Or become dog food." Because I knew their fears weren't completely baseless, I added, "When I find out where we're going, I'll send a text."

"Good girl." Donna started walking, taking us all with her. "I'm just editing pics tomorrow night so if you need me, I'm here."

"I'll be with Jacob," Becca said, "but if you need us, you know we'll be there."

Yes, I did. As goofy, annoying, and overprotective as they were, these ladies were my family.

"Thanks, guys. Love you all."

"Love you," echoed the four women before we all ended the chat.

Grateful they were in my life, I left the phone on the bed and shuffled into the bathroom. Sliding on a Pikachu headband, I slid my hair back from my face before reaching for my box of face masks. Examining my pores in the mirror, I mumbled, "Now to get rid of as many of you as I can."

CHAPTER TEN

In the two hours before the date, I changed clothes four times. To contrast this, the last time Fletcher and I went out to eat before the breakup, I wore leggings, a Naruto hoodie, and a DC Comics baseball cap. Maybe I *had* let the spark die a bit.

Despite the girls' agreement that I should wear jeans, I kept second-guessing and slipping into casual dresses, but most were ones I wore to work. Every time I looked in the mirror the words *boring librarian* screamed back at me. That wasn't the vibe I wanted to give so I conceded to my friends and switched back to jeans. I even found a somewhat stylish white denim jacket that I rarely wore in the back of the closet.

Giving myself a final check in the mirror, I tucked a loose strand of hair behind my ear before reaching for the lip gloss. As I smacked my lips together, my cell rang and

I rolled my eyes, knowing it was Josie. She'd have to wait for the date info until after Ryan picked me up. And then she'd still have to wait until I found a spare minute to send the text without giving the move away.

Snagging the phone off my dresser, I answered without looking at the screen. "I don't know yet, woman."

"Megan, it's Dad."

Oops. "Oh, sorry about that. I didn't look and thought you were Josie."

"That's okay. What don't you know yet?" he asked.

"I'm going on a date tonight, but I don't know where to yet."

"A date? How come you didn't tell me?"

I guess I should have called earlier, but today was laundry day. Between that and getting lost in my book for a couple of hours, I hadn't thought about it.

"He only asked me last night. It's a new guy on my softball team."

"Is he nice?"

An odd question, since I wasn't likely to go out with someone who wasn't nice, but then as the girls had pointed out, I didn't know him that well yet.

"Seems to be. What's up with you? Did you need something?"

Dad cleared his throat, which told me something serious was coming. "I'm calling to invite you to lunch tomorrow. I want you to meet Nessa."

Meet the girlfriend? I hadn't expected the moment to come so soon. Or so out of nowhere. I'd never say no, of course. The same elation he'd displayed while talking about her last weekend remained in his voice now. I wasn't exactly a little kid, but this still felt like a monumental moment. This could be the first time I meet my future stepmother.

Wow, did that sound strange in my head.

"I'd love to, Dad." Checking the clock as I passed through the living room to grab some shoes from the front closet, I saw that Ryan would arrive any minute. "Can you text me the details? I still need to get my shoes on and my date should be here soon."

"Of course, of course. Nessa is a little nervous about meeting you, but I told her she had nothing to worry about." He paused before adding, "She doesn't, does she?"

He was so cute.

"Nothing at all. If you like her, then I like her." Any woman smart enough to finally scoop him up after all these years won bonus points in my book. My doorbell rang, making my heart leap into my throat. "My date's here so I need to go. Message me all the details for tomorrow, and I'll be there."

"Will do, hon. Have a good time, but if you need me to come get you for any reason, just call."

I grabbed my purse and headed down the stairs. "Don't worry. The girls are already prepared to come to the rescue if needed." I had a virtual army ready to ride into battle over one innocent date. "Love you," I said without thinking as I swung the door open.

Ryan blinked over the threshold, clearly surprised by this greeting. "Hello to you, too?"

He looked so good I was smacked speechless for several seconds. The man cleaned up well. His jaw was clean-shaven, his hair brushed back but with a loose curl hovering over his left brow. He wore a light-pink button-down and dark-wash jeans over black leather shoes. Anyone who said a man had to be over six feet tall to look like a model had never seen Ryan Stallings heading out on a date.

Senses returning, I held my phone in the air. "No, no. Not you. I was just hanging up with my dad."

He visibly relaxed, and the slow smile softened his eyes. "Ah. Okay. Good to know." Motioning to the stairs, he said, "You ready?"

"I am." Stepping out, I pulled the door closed behind me and turned to lock it. "Since I didn't know where we were going, I wasn't sure what to wear. I hope this is all right."

Keeping his eyes on my face, he said, "You look great. I like your hair down like that."

That's right. He'd only seen me with it up at practices. Trying to ignore the blush warming my cheeks, I dropped my keys into my purse. "Thank you. You look good, too."

We descended the stairs together to his car parked at the curb, and I climbed inside when he opened the door for me. All of this chivalry was going to take some getting used to. Even on our first date, Fletcher hadn't opened the car door. I didn't consider it a slight since my arms were as capable as his, but the thoughtfulness was nice.

"So where are we going?" I asked once he joined me inside.

"Do you like Italian?" he asked.

"Isn't that a requirement of living in this city?" I replied.

He nodded to the side. "Seems that way. I haven't been here long, remember?"

I shifted in my seat to face him a little more. "That's right. Where did you move from?"

"Before here it was Chicago. Before that it was Milwaukee and Columbus."

"You get around." I didn't want to ask about his job lest he turn the questions back on me. Once we got through the date and I hopefully got him to like me, *then* I would correct the bookstore bit. "Are you the restless type then?"

"No." He shot me a half grin. "After college I jumped around a bit, trying to find my niche. A decade later I'm ready to put down some roots."

So he was a couple years older than I was. Not bad. With that baby face, he could also pass for much younger.

"Does Pittsburgh feel like a *putting down roots* kind of place?"

A bit early for me to be asking if he planned to stay in town, but I'd rather know now than after falling for him. It wasn't that I would never consider living anywhere else, but my friends were here. Dad was here. Pittsburgh felt like home.

"I like it so far," he said, making a left at the light. "Have you been to Scoglio in Greentree?"

A little fancier than I'd expected, but not so much that I'd feel underdressed.

"I've been there one time. A friend of mine is an event planner, and she checks out local restaurants to know what to recommend to clients when they have out-of-town guests or want to book a small rehearsal dinner. One of the perks of being her friend is that I get to tag along *and* I get a free meal out of it."

"I haven't been," Ryan said, "but I asked a buddy and he said this place is nice. Especially if I want to impress a girl." Before I could process that statement, he added, "You can go ahead and send it now if you want."

"Send what?"

"Where we're going."

Was I that obvious?

"I don't..."

"It's okay. I have a younger sister back in Akron, and anytime she goes out with a new guy, I tell her to make sure someone knows where she is the whole time." A

Hummer pulled out in front of us, and Ryan reacted quickly without any of the road rage I was used to from Lindsey. She really did need anger management classes. "You're on a date with a man you barely know," he said. "I get it."

"My friends did ask me to tell them where we were going," I confessed.

"Just to be clear, I'm not one of those guys. You have nothing to fear from me."

The girls might call me naive, but I absolutely believed him. That didn't mean I couldn't tease him a bit.

"To be fair, if you *were* one of those guys, isn't that exactly what you'd say?"

His laughter was deep and rich and became my new favorite sound. "Good point."

After waking my screen, I fired off the text. *We're going for Italian. It's all good, ladies. Enjoy your night.* Knowing what would follow, I silenced the phone and dropped it into my purse.

"So you're looking to impress me, huh?" I asked.

Ryan kept his eyes on the road. "That's the goal of a first date, right? To impress you enough to get a second one?"

Oh man, he was good. "I suppose so. You're doing pretty well so far."

Relief softened his expression, and I realized he might have been as nervous as I was. Cutting brown eyes my way, he said, "I'll try to keep that up."

A man willing to give some effort. What more could a girl ask for?

———

THE RESTAURANT SAT in an odd location in the back of a corporate complex. If I hadn't been there before, I might have worried Ryan really was taking me to some remote area to turn me into kibble. The plaza was mostly deserted, but the lot in front of the burgundy awning sporting the name Scoglio Restaurant Greentree was packed. Thankfully, we had a reservation and were seated within minutes.

The hostess let us know that Marianna, our waitress, would be with us shortly, then left us to peruse the menu.

"Since you've been here before, do you have any recommendations?" Ryan asked.

It'd been a couple of years and my memory of the food was dim at best. Though I did remember loving one dish in particular.

"The Chicken Picatta is really good. I think Becca enjoyed the lasagna as well."

"Is Becca your event planner friend?"

"She is." I reached for my water glass. "Weddings, retirements, graduations, corporate events. You name it and she plans it."

With a head tilt, he said, "That sounds really interesting, actually."

I didn't want to get too deep into the occupation discussion, so I changed the subject. "You said your sister is back in Akron. Is that where you're from?"

"Yeah, that's where I grew up. Rachel is twenty-four and just finished her master's in library science. You two would probably have a lot in common."

My heart stopped. Did he know? It wasn't as if no one on the team knew what I did for a living. Dang it, I should have thought of that. Someone must have told him. But then, was this date some elaborate gotcha moment?

"Why do you say that?"

Dark brows drew together. "Since you work in a bookstore, I just assumed you like books. Am I wrong?"

"Oh."

Guilt made it impossible to meet his gaze. I knew enough now to feel pretty confident Ryan wouldn't have any preconceived notions about my job, but the whole lie thing was a different story. Clearing that up sooner rather than later was probably a good idea.

"About tha—"

"Good evening," our waitress said as she stepped up to the table. Black hair pulled back in a low bun, she smiled, her green eyes darting between me and my date. "I'm Marianna and I'll be your server this evening. Have you dined with us before?"

"Megan has, but I haven't," Ryan replied.

"Well, Megan, I hope you had a positive experience

with us."

I nodded, my courage dwindling by the second. "Yes, the food was really good."

"Great. First up, then, can I get you some wine?"

Ryan looked at me with arched brows, waiting for me to reply first. At this point, I needed a little liquid courage.

"Pinot Grigio, please."

Marianna turned his way. "And you, sir?"

"I'll have the same, thank you."

"That's easy enough." The waitress rubbed her hands together. "Have you considered an appetizer? The stuffed banana peppers are a favorite. Or maybe a little fried calamari?"

"I was thinking about the stuffed mushroom caps," he said. "What do you want, Megan?"

I wanted the server to go away so I that could get this over with. "Anything you order is fine."

Tapping the list at the top of the menu, he said, "Let's go with the mushroom caps."

"Yes, sir." Marianna ducked to avoid bumping a waiter who passed carrying a large tray on his shoulder. "I'll put the order in and be right back with your wine."

"Thank you," said my date as I pretended to scan the menu. I was too distracted to focus on the words. I opened my mouth to try the confession again, but before I could speak, he said, "Did you grow up here in the city?"

"I was born in Uniontown, actually, but I moved here

after college, and Dad moved shortly after."

"What about your mom?"

My confession window was closing by the minute. "My mother hasn't been in my life since I was seven." If you didn't count the letter in my desk, which I was still ignoring. Did a letter qualify as *in* my life? Not really.

Ryan leaned his elbows on the edge of the table. "Is that a good or a bad thing?"

Excellent question. "A little of both."

"At the risk of being nosy, can I ask what happened?"

Not what I expected to talk about tonight, but maybe when I confessed to lying, he'd feel more lenient after the motherless child story.

"My parents were still teenagers when they had me. One careless night in the back seat of a Chevy led to a shotgun wedding, and I soon followed. Mom gave it seven years, but she had a wild streak and decided family life wasn't for her. She left for California, and I haven't seen her since."

Narrowed eyes watched me in silence and I felt as if he could see into my soul. "You don't feel as matter of fact about that as you sound, do you?"

I did before the stupid letter came. "That was a long time ago. Dad gave me a great childhood. He's the best parent a girl could ask for."

"Not really an answer to my question." Leaning back, Ryan said, "I have a similar story."

He sighed and I leaned forward. "You don't have to

share just because I did."

"I don't mind. I was with my mom until I was around one or so, though I don't remember her. She left me with a nun at St. Ignatius Catholic Church and said she'd be back in a couple of hours." He paused and then shrugged. "You can guess the rest."

Wait. What about his sister?

"Did she leave Rachel, too?"

"Rachel isn't my blood sister. Our parents adopted me when I was three. They'd tried but couldn't have kids. Four years later, Mom got pregnant with Rachel. She's their miracle baby."

What did that make him?

"Did that change how they treated you?"

"Oh, no," he said, waving his hands. "They gave me a great life and never treated me any differently."

I couldn't imagine leaving a baby like that. He must have been so scared. At least I'd had Dad. I wasn't left with strangers, which is what might have happened if she'd taken me with her.

"Do you ever wonder what happened to her?" I asked. "Your birth mother?"

"I don't have to wonder. She found me a few years ago."

What were the chances that he and I could have this much in common? "How did that go?" Ryan hesitated and I realized I'd asked too much. "I'm sorry. You don't have to answer that."

With a shake of his head, he said, "It's all right." Rubbing a hand along his smooth jaw, his gaze locked on his water glass. "At first I wanted nothing to do with her. She left me, you know?" Did I ever. "But then I thought about how differently my life might have been if she'd kept me. She was barely sixteen when I was born. In a desperate moment she picked a safe place where she knew I'd be cared for, and I was. My parents are really good people. I can't imagine not having them in my life. When I took all of that into consideration, forgiving her just made sense."

I did not feel that generous toward Geraldine. She might have been young when I was born, but that had not been the case when she left. I wasn't a baby who wouldn't remember her. I remembered *everything*. And I'd blamed myself for years. She made me feel defective. Unlovable. Unwanted. There was nothing she could say that would undo all of those things.

"Do you have a relationship with her now?" I asked.

"I know where she is. I've met the half-siblings that she had after me, and we've gotten together in person a couple of times, but we don't talk every day or anything."

There was no way that I had half-siblings floating out there somewhere. Geraldine had made it abundantly clear that she was not cut out to be a mother.

"Have you *ever* heard from your mom?" Ryan asked, but the waitress returned with our wine and appetizer before I could answer.

"This is hot so be careful," Marianna said as she lowered the plate onto the table. "Are you ready to order your entrees or do you need more time?"

I hadn't even looked through the whole menu yet. "Could we get a couple minutes?"

"Of course. Take your time."

Distracted, I didn't pay much attention to the food until he said, "These are even better than I thought they'd be. You've got to try one."

Mushrooms weren't my favorite, but I didn't mind them. Lifting one into my mouth, I chewed twice before a piece of something slid down my throat. Within seconds, my cheeks grew hot and my throat thickened. Panic setting in, I looked at what was left of the mushroom in my hand and there it was. A piece of shrimp.

"Oh no," I mumbled, but speaking was already growing difficult.

"What is it?" Ryan said, his eyes widening. "Why are your cheeks so red? Megan?"

I dropped the food and spit what was left in my mouth onto the small plate before me. Throat quickly closing, I cleared the smaller bits out of my cheeks.

"Are you choking?" he said, rising from his chair and coming around to my side of the table.

I needed to get this out before it was too late.

Shaking my head furiously, I gripped the table. "I'm allergic to shellfish."

CHAPTER ELEVEN

I HAD NEVER BEEN SO MORTIFIED *IN MY LIFE.*

Thankfully, I'd been able to get the auto-injector from my purse, but not before the hostess, three waiters, three fellow diners, and a busboy surrounded our table. One woman was calling out for a doctor. Another kept saying I needed the Heimlich. Ryan ignored them all, rolled back my chair, and stuck the medicine in my thigh. Now our food—which we did not have to pay for—was in to-go boxes on the back seat while we rode in silence back to my house.

"I'm really sorry," I said for the fourth time. I'd ruined the meal, the date, and the entire night.

"Megan, seriously. You don't need to apologize. I'm the one who ordered the mushrooms and told you to eat one."

"I should have read the description in the menu."

"It's an honest mistake." Sending me a concerned glance, he said, "Are you sure you're okay? I can still take you to the ER."

Wouldn't that be a topper on the night? I would already have a hard time explaining this to the girls without adding a trip to the hospital at the end.

"A little Benadryl and I'll be fine." Eyes closed, a realization dawned, and I laughed.

"What's so funny?" he asked.

"Maybe my friends were right to worry. I did almost die on this date."

Ryan did not see the humor. "You really scared me back there."

I supposed not everyone was used to this sort of thing. "I'm sorry. I know it isn't funny, but if I don't laugh, I'll cry, and I'm trying not to do that in front of you."

He took my hand in his and rubbed a thumb over my knuckle. "You deserve to cry after that. I might join you."

Genuine laughter burst from my lips, and I squeezed his fingers. "I'm still humiliated but thank you."

"You have nothing to be embarrassed about. Think of it this way, we'll always have a great story to tell about our first date."

That he called it our first date and not our only date was encouraging. He pulled the car up to the curb in front of my porch and I undid my seat belt. When he undid his, I said, "What are you doing?"

"I'm not leaving you alone," he said before climbing out of the car.

Not that I wanted the night to end, but I was certain my lips were still swollen, *and* I couldn't remember in what state I'd left the apartment. Definitely not in bring-a-man-home condition, I knew that.

"You don't have to do this," I said once he opened the passenger door. "I'll be fine."

"Megan, you could have died less than an hour ago. I'm not going to drop you off, and then leave."

"But—"

"No buts." He held up his right hand. "I solemnly swear that I have no ulterior motives. I'll even stand by the door if you want, but I'm not leaving."

Being alone right away probably wasn't a good idea. "Okay, but I have to warn you that my apartment is a mess."

He flashed a boy-next-door grin while the streetlights twinkled in his eyes. "Unless you're talking hoarder level, I'm sure I can handle it." Taking my hand, he helped me out of the car. "Are you okay to walk on your own?"

My knees were a little shaky so I took a second to steady them. Nodding, I said, "I can do it."

"I know you're strong, but lean on me if you need to."

That was quite possibly the best thing a man had ever said to me. "Where did you come from?" I said, feeling as if I'd located the one living manicorn on the planet.

"Akron?" he said.

"That must be a magical place."

"No one would ever call Akron, Ohio, magical."

They would if they were on this date.

———

I MANAGED NOT to lean on him for support until we were halfway up the stairs. Turns out having your airway cut off for even a few seconds left you a little woozy. Unable to remember exactly how the apartment looked, I braced for the mess at the top of the stairs, but the place wasn't so bad. The bedroom was worse, I knew, since I'd tossed countless outfits onto the bed, but at least out here in the little living room and kitchen area, the clutter was minimal.

True to his word, Ryan didn't step a foot beyond the door to the apartment while I moved some mail and my laptop from the couch to the coffee table. "You can sit down," I said as I fluffed the throw pillows. "Do you want something to drink?"

"I don't want to be any trouble," he said, lingering with his hands in his pockets.

For heaven's sake. He'd just saved my life. The least I could do was give the man some water. "Don't be silly." I remembered that our food was still in the car. I might not feel like eating, but that didn't mean he had to go hungry. "You need to go get the food so you can eat."

"Are you hungry?" he asked, as if I'd given this suggestion for my own benefit.

"No, but you need to have dinner. You don't have to starve on my account."

Jaw set, he shook his head. "I'm not going to let you watch me eat."

"Ryan, seriously. You were looking forward to that meal. There's no sense in wasting it." Holding out a hand, I added, "Give me your keys and I'll go get it."

Looking highly insulted, he ignored my request. "You barely made it up the stairs a minute ago. I'll go get the food."

I was actually feeling better already, but I didn't argue. While he was gone, I took the allergy medicine and then brought in a plate and silverware from the kitchen. Scoglio's food was too good to eat out of a paper box with plastic utensils. Laying out a nice setting on the coffee table, I stepped back and thought of one more finishing touch. After a quick dash back to the kitchen, which was mere feet from the sofa, I returned with a lighter in hand and lit my three-wick ocean-scented candle. As Ryan returned, I hurled the lighter onto the desk and plopped onto the couch, pretending I hadn't been creating a subtly romantic setting.

Not that I was trying to woo him into anything beyond a nice chat, but this was still part of the date. I'd rather he remember the night for something more than my near-death experience.

He stopped when he spotted the table. "What did you do?"

Doubts kicked in. Was I being too obvious? Trying too hard? "I just got a plate and some silverware so you can eat."

"And lit a candle."

Leaning forward, I blew out the flames. "Nope. No candle."

He set the bag from the restaurant on the table before sliding the candle farther away. "I appreciate the gesture, but if you kept that lit, I'd need to steal some of your allergy medicine. Sorry."

Relief flooded through me. "Thank goodness. I was afraid you thought I was trying to seduce you." The moment the words were out I dropped my head into my hands. "I can't believe I just said that out loud."

"You could try," he said with an even tone, "but I'm not that easy."

Was he serious? His expression was unreadable as he pulled containers of food from the bag. After letting me squirm for a full twenty seconds, he paused and shot me a grin. "I'm kidding, Megan. You're really cute when you're flustered."

He was cute all the time, the jerk. Kicking off my shoes under the table, I tucked my legs beneath my bottom and leaned on the sofa arm. "You're an agitator, aren't you?"

"I'll plead the fifth on that one." Popping open a

small container, he quickly closed it again. "Someone didn't get the memo. These go in the garbage."

"What is it?"

"The mushrooms. I told the hostess we didn't need them." Sitting back down, he opened the next container. "This is your Chicken Picatta. Are you sure you don't want some now?"

I *was* a bit hungry, and my throat felt much better.

"I could eat a little bit. Let me get a fork."

When I returned, Ryan took the plate from my hand and used his fork to dish up half of the container. He handed the plate back before moving on to his Pork Chop Valdostana. Once he'd neatly served himself and then closed and stacked the containers, he sat back and rested the heavy plate on his chest.

"I'm sorry I don't have a kitchen table," I said. "There's just nowhere to put one in here."

"I eat most of my meals like this. Growing up, we weren't a *sit down to dinner and talk about your day* kind of family. Between my sports, Rachel's piano lessons, Dad working second shift, and Mom driving us kids all over the place, meals were quick and casual."

That sounded hectic, but nice. A full family unit all going in their own directions but together when they could be.

"Did you play anything other than baseball?" I asked.

"Around middle school I did all three—baseball, football, and basketball. Then most of the guys hit growth sports and by junior year, size became an issue." There was no pity-me or bruised ego in his tone. "I was built for baseball, and that's where I put my focus."

Resting the plate on my bent knee, I said, "You aren't short though."

A dark brow arched high. "Not to you, maybe, but five foot eight is below average when it comes to men's sports."

He had a point. Personally, I preferred baseball to the other two. Way less contact which meant far fewer injuries.

"How young were you when you started playing softball?" he asked.

"Eight," I replied. "I think Dad was trying to find a distraction from the missing mother stuff. We tried piano lessons, but I have zero musical abilities. Then there was ballet, but the instructor said I was too old by that point."

Ryan nearly choked. "Eight was too old?"

"To be a beginner, yeah. I didn't mind. Tutus and toe shoes were not my thing either."

"But softball was?"

I pointed at the cluttered bookshelves around the room. "As you can see, I'm a book person. As a kid, if I wasn't at school, I was in my room reading. But the first time I hit the ball, I got this crazy rush of adrenaline, and I've been playing ever since."

"Did it work then?"

Now he'd lost me. "Did what work?"

"As a distraction from your mom leaving."

A question I hadn't thought of before. "Yes and no. While I was on the field, I could focus and forget that there was a hole in my family. But then the game would end, and the moms would gather near the bench to pick up their kids." I shoved a piece of chicken around my plate. "Dad was always there so it wasn't like I had no one. I just wished she would've been there."

"I get that," he said, and we fell into companionable silence.

I thought of the letter tucked into the drawer a few feet away. Thought about how badly I wanted that letter twenty years ago. How I'd longed for any sign that she thought of me. That she would come back and we would be a family again. All of which made me feel disloyal to Dad.

"When I first heard from my birth mother," Ryan said, "I got really angry. Like if she didn't want to be in my life back then, what gave her the right to come back all those years later."

The man was reading my mind. "But you still met with her. Why?"

He sat up and lowered the plate to his lap. "I wanted answers. I stopped questioning her motives and decided that I deserved to know what happened. Why she did what she did."

That's what I'd been doing for the last week. Trying to guess what Geraldine wanted from me. I hadn't stopped to even consider that I might want something from her.

Without a word, I set my plate on the coffee table and crossed the short distance to the desk. Pulling the letter from the drawer, I returned to the couch and set the envelope between us.

"What is that?" Ryan asked when I held silent.

"I got this last Friday. It's from my mother." As if I'd set a live grenade on the sofa cushion, Ryan went still. "I haven't opened it," I added.

"Why not?" When I didn't answer, he said, "Okay, that's a stupid question. What do you think is in there?"

"I don't know. I've come up with countless scenarios in my head. She needs money. She's ill and having regrets." Pulling my feet up, I hugged my knees and rattled off the one I'd come up with a few days ago. "She needs a kidney and I'm her only living relative."

"Are you?"

"Her only relative?" I shrugged. "I assume so. She was an only child and her parents died when I was a baby. If there's some distant cousins out there, I don't know about them."

Silence reigned again until he set his plate next to mine on the table. "Have you thought about having someone else read it first?"

Interesting idea. "Are you volunteering?"

"I can't claim to be an impartial bystander, since I care enough not to want what's in that envelope to hurt you, but I also know what you're going through. When my letter came, I let my mom read it first."

The idea had merit. This could be like going through the experience with a seasoned guide. Someone who'd been there, done that. Then again, he was supposed to be my date, not my therapist.

"I'm sure you didn't bargain for any of this when you asked me to dinner."

"If you mean I never guessed the date would be this interesting, then yeah," he replied. "But that's a good thing."

"It's a good thing that I gave you a heart attack at dinner, and now I'm considering putting a twenty-three-year weight on your shoulders?"

A gentle smile curved his lips. "I'm the one who offered, but no pressure. If you aren't ready, put the letter back in the drawer until you are. There are no rules for this stuff."

I stared at the envelope, debating what to do. Putting it off would only mean my imagination running away with more outlandish possibilities. I'd opted not to read it because I wasn't going to give her the power to affect my life, but that's exacting what was happening anyway. Better to get it over with.

Hopping to my feet, I snagged the letter opener from a cup on the desk. Handing it over, I took a deep breath and said, "Let's do it."

CHAPTER TWELVE

"Wait," I said as he slid the opener under the flap. "Hold on."

Ryan stopped in mid motion. "Are you changing your mind?"

I perched on the edge of the cushion. "No, I just need to take a few more deep breaths." Breathing in and out, I emptied my lungs one more time. "Okay, now I'm ready."

He waited, as if testing to see if I'd stop him again. When I held silent, he cut the envelope open. Pulling out the letter, he said, "You're sure you're good with me reading it first?"

A nod was the best I could do as all the moisture from my mouth had gone to my palms.

In silence, he unfolded the lined paper and scanned the words. There was only one sheet, and there were no words on the back. That meant no lengthy explanations or long pleas for my forgiveness. When his eyes reached the bottom of the page, he flipped it over, and then back, his jaw tight.

"Well?" I said, about to jump out of my skin.

One dark brow arched high. "You aren't her only living relative," Ryan said.

I popped to my feet. "What?"

"There's no request for money, or any of the other things you suggested earlier. But she does have a request."

Why did he look so annoyed? "A request? For what?"

Ryan held the letter out. "You should read it."

I didn't feel good about this. "I'm not giving her anything. If that's all that's in there, then forget it. I'll just throw it away."

"No," he said. "You *need* to read it, Megan."

Rubbing my palms on my thighs, I stared at the single sheet of paper. This was the moment. Shaking out my hands, I stood and paced away, then came back and sat again. "Okay, I can do this."

Letter in hand, I read in silence.

Dear Megan,

This is your mother. I'm sure you're surprised to hear from me, but know that I wouldn't be writing this letter if it wasn't important. I've learned that my daughter, Cassandra, is there in Pittsburgh attempting to research my past. She told her brother that she's been working at a local library, and your name came up. She has no idea who you are, and I'd like to keep it that way. I long ago left the person I was behind, and I don't want that history coming to light now. Please do what you can to dissuade Cassandra from pursuing this further. If you cannot stop her entirely, at least keep her from finding the information she's looking for.

Thank you,

Geraldine

Numb, I stared at the words until they blurred on the page. She had another daughter. And a son. Children that she'd raised while I'd been left behind, wondering what I'd done wrong. Why she hadn't wanted me.

I had siblings.

"Cassie," I said, realizing who the letter was about.

"Do you know her?" Ryan asked.

I looked up. "She's been working at the library for a week or so. We talked the other day, and she said she and her mother don't get along. That she refused to share anything about her life before Cassie was born, so she came here to find the answers herself." Glancing back to the letter, I muttered, "But for some reason Cassie's last name is O'Malley. I never would have suspected we're related."

Ryan leaned forward, his elbows on his knees. "Are you going to do what she asks?"

Was I? Just because she'd given birth to me didn't mean I owed her anything. She hadn't even apologized for leaving. For abandoning me. In fact, she made me sound like some dirty little secret that needed to stay that way. Was she ashamed of me? I deserved better than that. Dad deserved better than that. And Cassie deserved her answers.

"No, I'm not. I'm going to do the exact opposite."

"I don't blame you," he said, "but you might want to think about this. As you just found out, learning you have a sibling is a big revelation. You won't just be telling Cassie you exist. You'll be telling her that her mother *abandoned a child*. If they're already on rough terms, news like that isn't going to help."

Why would I want to help? Cassie deserved to know the truth. But I did need to think about *how* to do this.

"I'll find a better way to tell her than I just found out, but I won't help Geraldine keep this from her. Two decades is long enough." I folded the letter and slid it back into the envelope. "I feel like an idiot for not opening this sooner."

Ryan reached for my plate before picking up his own and getting to his feet. "Don't beat yourself up. You had good reason for putting it off."

"What are you doing?" I asked as he walked over to the kitchen.

"I assume you have a microwave over here," he said, finding the appliance in the corner of the counter. "We're going to start this meal over again, and we aren't doing it with cold food."

This man really liked do-overs. I pushed off the couch to join him in the kitchen. "I can do that."

Ignoring me, he slid my plate into the microwave, tapped a couple of buttons, and hit start. "Your dinner will be served in forty-five seconds." Leaning his back to the counter, he crossed his arms and watched me with a narrowed gaze.

Not sure what was happening, I tried not to squirm. "What?" I finally said.

Ryan shook his head. "I'm trying to figure out why Fletcher would have been stupid enough to let you go."

Did I give him the real reason? I mean, this date was likely to give him false notions about my life. Like, that I had one. Since I'd already stretched the truth about my job, I decided not to compound the lies. In fact, this was a good way to test what his reaction to the truth of that might be.

"He used the old *we're too different* cliché, but what he really meant was that I'm too boring for him to be with."

Dark brows arched high. "Too boring?

I nodded. "Yes."

"What does he want? A circus act?"

"That might work for him, actually." I laughed, but for some reason felt the need to defend him. "He just likes excitement and being social."

The microwave dinged and Ryan turned to retrieve my food. Setting it on the counter next to me, he said,

"Make sure that's warm enough." While I stirred the noodles, he put his own dish in the microwave. "You know why Fletcher is like that, right?"

As far as I knew, the two men were virtual strangers. "It's just who he is, I guess."

With pursed lips, he shook his head. "He's insecure."

Fletcher insecure? That was ridiculous. "Trust me when I tell you that no one thinks as highly of Fletcher Howard as Fletcher does."

"It's an act," Ryan insisted. "He needs constant outside validation because he doesn't actually like himself at all."

Was that possible? Had the problem really been him and not me? If so, what did that say about how long I stayed and never noticed what was really happening?

"You barely know him," I pointed out.

"True. I'm only going by my brief interactions with him and what you've told me, but I stand by the assessment." Flashing that sexy grin of his, he added, "Also, I might have minored in psychology in college, and Fletcher Howard is a textbook example of the insecure male. The car. The need for attention. His breaking up with you but not wanting to see you go out with someone else."

Some of this was making sense. I'd taken a psychology class myself, though I'd never attempted to apply the basics I'd learned to the men I'd dated. Duh. That would have been a smart thing to do.

"Now I feel sorry for him."

The microwave dinged again and Ryan spun to open it. "If he's lucky, he'll find the right person and eventually learn to feel better about himself." Which meant I had not been the right person. I wasn't sure how to feel about that. "Is yours good?" he asked.

I touched the noodles in the center of the plate and said, "Maybe another thirty seconds for the pasta."

"I can do that."

While the food was switched around again, I felt a strong desire to get my confession over with. "We haven't talked much about our jobs."

"Now that's a boring subject," he said. "How about we watch a movie?"

Not the reaction I expected. I needed an opening to this topic and he wasn't making it easy. "I doubt your job is boring. I'd love to hear about it."

"It's just a bunch of numbers. I'd put you to sleep within minutes." The timer went off and Ryan handed over my plate. "See if this is better."

I tested the food and found it heated through. "Yes, this is good."

"Then are we ready for dinner and a movie?" he asked.

I could always confess after the movie. Grabbing two bottles of pop from the fridge, I said, "Let's do it."

———

As the sun penetrated my eyelids, I felt something pressing against my back. Not quite awake, I stretched and my toes hit something hard as memories of the night before floated back. The scene at the restaurant. The letter. Ryan and I watching a movie. I recalled leaning my head on his shoulder as Bruce Willis dangled from the side of a building. After that, there was nothing.

Realization dawned. I fell asleep on him.

Opening one eye, I spotted the TV beyond the coffee table and my fears were confirmed. Then I realized I had no idea if Ryan was still there. He definitely wasn't on the couch with me, and I couldn't imagine he'd sleep in my bed and leave me out here on the sofa. Just in case, I checked the floor.

I was alone.

With a groan, I pushed up and swung my feet onto the carpet. The Winnie the Pooh Christmas blanket that was usually draped over the chair in the corner bunched around my hips. As I shoved the hair out of my eyes, I spotted a sticky note on a pop bottle and snatched it off.

Megan,

Thanks for a great night. I hope we can do it again. Without the shellfish this time.

Talk soon,

Ryan

I didn't even get to say goodbye. Spinning, I checked the clock on the wall. Nearly noon. I couldn't remember the last time I'd slept so late. Maybe he'd sent a text by now to check on me. Head still foggy, I tried to remember where I put my phone. I hadn't used it since we were on our way to the restaurant more than twelve hours ago.

Oh no. This was not going to be good.

Finding my purse near the door, I tapped the screen to find countless notifications. The top one was from Josie.

If you do not call me within five minutes, I'm coming to your house.

The message was sent thirty minutes before.

As if on cue, my doorbell started ringing nonstop. I understood they were worried, but this kind of drama was not necessary.

"I'm coming," I yelled as I hurried down the stairs. Swinging the door open, I said, "Lay off the bell already."

To my surprise, all four of my friends were on my doorstep, and none of them looked happy to see me.

"What the hell, Megan?" snapped Josie.

"We were worried sick," added Becca.

"I told you she was fine," said Donna as Lindsey pushed past all of them.

"Are you okay?" she asked, cupping my cheeks, then checking my arms for bruises, I assumed. "Did he knock you out? Drug you?" She looked up the stairs. "Is the bastard still here?"

Brushing her hands away, I rubbed the sleep from my eyes. "He isn't here, and none of that happened. I fell asleep while we were watching a movie, and just woke up. He must have tossed a blanket over me and left."

"Is that all he did?" Josie asked.

They really needed to get their imaginations in check. "Guys, look at me. I'm fine. Ryan was a complete gentleman, and he stuck around when most guys would have dropped me on the curb and run."

"Why?" Becca asked. "What happened?"

In desperate need of a toothbrush and the chance to empty my bladder, I turned to head upstairs. "Just come up and I'll tell you everything." My overprotective friends followed and once inside the apartment, I said, "Give me a minute. I'll be right back."

I took care of the necessities in the bathroom, then returned feeling more awake. Josie, Becca, and Donna all sat on the couch while Lindsey occupied one of the chairs. I settled into the other and debated on where to begin.

"Last night was a bit… eventful."

"Good eventful or bad eventful?" Donna asked.

I started at the beginning. "I accidentally ate a piece of shrimp at dinner."

"Oh, shit," said Lindsey as Becca scooted forward on the sofa. "Are you all right?" she asked. "Did you have your injector?"

"Yes, I had it, and thankfully Ryan knew how to use it because I was barely able to get it out of my purse let alone inject myself."

"That's a point in his favor." But Josie wasn't appeased. "Did he take you to the hospital?"

"There was no need for that. It was a tiny bite and I took Benadryl when I got home." Which explained why I'd fallen asleep. I should have known that would happen. "But that isn't all that happened."

"I knew it," said Lindsey, leaping to her feet. "What did he do? No one touch anything so we don't contaminate the evidence."

We all stared at her in silence until Becca said, "I'm canceling your cable subscription. And your Netflix." To me, she said, "Go on, Meg."

I picked up the envelope from the coffee table. "I read the letter from my mother."

Lindsey dropped back into her chair. "What does it say?"

I handed it over. "Read it for yourself."

Becca read the letter out loud, and when she was finished, we all sat in silence for several seconds.

"You have siblings," Donna said in a hushed voice.

"Seems so."

Lindsey leaned back and crossed her arms. "She didn't even apologize for leaving."

"Or for ignoring you for twenty years," Josie added.

As if in shock, they all watched me with wide eyes. "Are you okay?" Becca asked.

Was I? I hadn't spent a lot of time processing the situation yet. Geraldine expressed no regret or remorse for what she'd done. In fact, she made it sound as if we'd simply agreed to go our separate ways. No harm, no foul, have a nice life. As if I hadn't been a little girl confused and heartbroken and left wondering why my mother didn't love me enough to stay in my life.

How unfeeling could a woman be?

"I'm angry," I said. "Not only does she want to keep *my existence* a secret, but she thinks I'd help her do it."

"Do you know this Cassandra person she's talking about?" Josie asked.

Nodding, I said, "A young woman has been doing some family research at the library lately. Her name is Cassie so I'm sure that's her."

Josie leaned forward. "Do you think she knows who you are?"

I took the letter from Becca and stuffed it back into the envelope. "I don't think so. We've talked and if she knows, she's a really good actress."

"That is so crazy," Becca said. "I mean, what are the odds?"

"How did she know your address?" Lindsey asked. We all looked her way. "She hasn't sent you anything since you were ten. How did Geraldine know where to send that letter?"

Stunned by the question, I said, "I don't know. An internet search, maybe? None of us are hard to find these days."

Lindsey didn't look convinced. "That's true, but the

tone of that letter doesn't sound like she had to work hard to find you."

"What are you saying? That she's been keeping tabs on me?"

My friend shrugged. "Maybe."

I'd always assumed that once she left, she never looked back. But then I'd also assumed that she'd never had more kids and I was clearly mistaken about that.

"What are you going to do?" asked Donna. "Will you tell Cassie who you are?"

This one I could answer. "I plan to. I'm just not sure how to do it yet. How do you tell a person that not only are you her sister, but that her mother left you and never came back?"

A collective silence fell over the room, and I didn't blame them. Who could possibly answer that?

"Do you know how old this girl is?" asked Lindsey.

"I'd guess in her early twenties," I said, tossing the letter onto the coffee table. "I've never asked."

"Geraldine left you twenty-three years ago, right?"

"It'll be twenty-three years in November." Recognizing the look on her face, I said, "Why?"

The amateur sleuth wannabe held my gaze in silence before saying, "Do the math. If this woman is twenty-two or older…"

The possibilities clicked into place. "Then she's Dad's daughter, too."

"We don't know that," Becca cut in. "And there's no reason to assume."

"She might only be twenty, right?" Josie watched me with wide eyes. "I mean, Geraldine wouldn't have—"

"The woman left a seven-year-old without a second thought," Donna said. "I wouldn't put anything past her."

This was getting more complicated by the second. With Dad happily finding love again, I'd been thinking of leaving him out of this entirely, but I couldn't do that if Cassie was his daughter. And thinking of Dad reminded me of our conversation before the date.

"Crap. I'm supposed to meet his girlfriend today." Scrambling, I found my phone and after dismissing a ton of messages from the girls, I located the one from Dad. Lunch was at his place at one. I checked the clock on the wall. "I have less than an hour to get ready and get over there. I need to hurry."

The girls all jumped up and Donna asked, "Are you going to tell him what was in the letter?"

"I'll have to eventually, but not today. He's finally moving on and I don't want anything from Geraldine to mess this up for him."

"Fair enough," said Josie. After kissing me on the check, she added, "Let us know how it goes."

"I will." I walked them to the door and waited until they were down the stairs and outside before hurrying into the bathroom. My lips were no longer swollen, but my hair was a mess and sleeping in mascara had left heavy black smudges beneath my eyes. Staring at my reflection, I pictured Cassie in my mind, searching for a resemblance.

Where my eyes were brown, hers were blue. My hair was dark while hers leaned more toward blond. That could be dyed, of course. Resemblance or not, she was my sister. Getting through today without sharing the revelation with Dad would be hard, but his happiness came first. Today was about him and Nessa, and Geraldine would stay in the past where she belonged. At least, for now.

CHAPTER THIRTEEN

"I'M HERE!" I CALLED AS I RUSHED INTO DAD'S HOUSE fifteen minutes late. I'd sent a text before leaving home to say that I was running behind.

Dad lived in a row house on a quiet street on the South Side, and finding a place to park had taken an extra minute. He'd been in this house since moving to the city after I had eight years ago. Becca and Lindsey had both grown up in the area so after college graduation, Josie and I basically followed them home. Donna didn't join the group until a year or two later when she and Becca met through work.

The narrow home, originally built in 1900, had a brick exterior painted mint green with mauve accents around the door and windows. It screamed city charm and I hoped to one day own something similar.

"Hey there, pumpkin," Dad said, greeting me as I stepped into the tiny living room. "How was your date?"

That was a long story for another day. "It was nice. I'm sorry I'm late."

He waved the apology away. "You're fine." Lowering his voice, he said, "Nessa is very nervous to meet you so she might come on a little strong at first. She'll calm down if you just give her a minute."

I wasn't sure what *come on strong* meant. "She doesn't need to be nervous with me."

"I told her that, but she knows you've had me all to yourself for a long time. Just let her get it out of her system." Bracing myself for the unknown, I followed him into the kitchen. "We're sitting outside. Do you want a soda?"

"Sure, I'll take one."

Dad grabbed a Pepsi from the fridge and we headed out to the patio. His warning had not been enough to prepare me for what followed.

"There you are!" shouted a slender woman, leaping from her patio chair and running to close the short distance between us. Dad's patio was only ten-by-ten feet and the table and umbrella took up most of that space. "I'm so happy to meet you!"

Twig-like arms pulled me into a hug, squeezing me tight enough to cut off my airway. A second later, she released me, pushing me away just enough to grip my upper arms. Her face, angular and slightly wrinkled, was entirely too close to mine, and her bright-blue eyes looked enormous, magnified by the thick lenses of her glasses, which were far too large for the size of her face.

Brown and silver curls darted out in every direction from her head, while bright-pink lips stretched wide to reveal a smile that was as oddly oversized as the glasses she wore. Nessa Broneicki looked like a Muppet.

Stunned speechless, I stared in silence until Dad said, "Megan, this is Nessa."

Right. I'd figured that part out. "Hi," I said before recovering enough to add, "It's nice to meet you."

"I've heard so much about you that I feel like we know each other already," she said, her voice locked at top levels. My ears were starting to ring. "I hope we can be good friends."

I wanted to like her. I really did. But holy wow was she a lot to take.

"Why don't we sit down?" Dad said as I stood motionless, not sure what to do next. Nessa was still gripping my arms and I feared she might pull me into another lung-crushing hug.

"Yes," she said. "Of course!" We each took a seat around the glass-top table with Dad across from me and Nessa to my right. She gripped my hand while hovering on the edge of her chair. "You're so lucky to have a daddy like James. He's such a caring man."

On this we could agree, but I wasn't used to this level of physical contact with a stranger. "He's the best dad a girl could ask for," I said, sliding my hand out of hers and into my lap. I tried to remember what he'd told me about her, but all I could recall was the wicked stepmother-like details. "He says you have two daughters?"

"I do," she said, her smile widening, which hadn't seemed possible. "My oldest is Nancy, and she lives in New York City with her partner Jasmine. They're getting married this Christmas. Then there's Beatrice, but we call her Bunnie. She and her husband live out in Dormont, and they have the most adorable little boy you'll ever meet. Maddox is my pride and joy."

Bunnie? That would be easy enough to remember. A million questions ran through my mind, but none felt appropriate to ask upon first meeting. Things like was her ex-husband—presuming she ever had one—still around? What were her intentions toward my father? Was she financially stable, and did she have a volume knob?

"So you two work together?"

"Nessa has been with the company for twenty-eight years," Dad said. "She practically runs the accounting department."

Blushing, she tapped Dad affectionately on the arm. "Don't be telling tales, now. I'm a worker bee at best. They'd never put me in charge of anything important."

This modesty did not sit well with Dad. "Nonsense. They couldn't function without you. Just last week Malcolm Turner told me he doesn't know what they're going to do when you retire. They're already dreading having to find a replacement."

"Are you retiring soon?" I asked.

"Not for a couple more years. I want to get to an even thirty, and then I plan to turn in my access key and start traveling."

That would put her barely into her early fifties, based on what Dad had told me. Retiring at that age was a distant dream for most people.

As if reading my mind, Dad said, "Nessa is a genius with numbers. She has the best retirement portfolio I've ever seen, and I've put together hundreds of them over the years."

He and Josie had had many spirited conversations about investment portfolios. When the subject of numbers came up, my eyes glazed over.

"I was afraid I was going to have to spend all that money by myself." Nessa's voice finally dropped to a tolerable level as she stared at Dad with sappy smile. "I don't worry about that now."

Wait. Whoa. Were they already at the point of spending their golden years together? He said they'd been dating for two months. This was moving entirely too fast.

A timer dinged from inside the house and Dad leaped from his chair. "That's the meatloaf. I'll be right back."

Oh, no. He was going to leave me alone with her. I considered offering to help, but that would be too obvious.

Once Dad stepped inside, Nessa said, "He's such a wonderful man." There was a quiet reverence in her tone. Enough to make me wonder where the loud woman I'd met a few minutes ago had gone. "He never stops talking about you."

Assuming that must get annoying, I said, "Sorry about that."

"Oh, no, no. I love it. I talk about my girls all the time, too. I've dated enough men over the years to know most of them don't want to hear about my kids. Your father is different. He's one of the good ones."

Yes, he was. "You know he hasn't dated in a long time, right?"

As if morphing into a new, more relaxed person, Nessa leaned back in her chair. "I do, and I'm glad for it. If another woman had snapped him up before now, I'd be missing out on something very special."

Maybe we *were* going to be friends. I just had to make a few things clear. "He's been really hurt in the past. I don't want him to go through anything like that ever again."

Acknowledging the message, she sat up and rested her arms on the table. "I promise you that I won't ever hurt him, Megan. I know a good thing when I find one."

Appeased, at least for now, I accepted her words. "That's good to know."

———

THE REST of the Sunday visit went well, and once Nessa calmed down, she was actually a very pleasant woman. Funny, too. She doted on Dad, who beamed when she was in the room. They were both practical yet nerdy enough to be adorable together. I got to see countless pictures of Maddox on Nessa's phone, and Dad dragged out a photo album from when I was a teenager. From braces to my first pom poms to the day I received my acceptance letter to Penn State, the images took me back in time to when Dad had been my whole world. The one person who would always be there no matter what.

Every photo sparked a story, and Dad remembered everything. When they were taken. What we were doing. Little details about something I'd said that day or where we'd gone to eat. Nessa listened intently to every tale and asked questions that triggered even more stories. For a couple of hours, I forgot about the letter and the library, and it wasn't until I was alone with Dad helping him load the dishwasher that I considered mentioning what I'd learned from Geraldine's letter. Part of me wanted his advice on how to tell Cassie of our connection. At the same time, that was a burden I couldn't bear to place on his shoulders.

He was happy again. I didn't want to do anything to wipe the smile from his face. So I kept the letter to myself.

Once at home for the night, I'd considered an array of options for how to talk to Cassie. I'd even done an internet search to see if there was some recommended way to tell a person that you were their sibling. A long shot, but I was desperate enough to try anything. The only decision I'd come to was that I didn't want to do it in the library. I'd have to see if Cassie would meet me someplace in the evening. Someplace quiet since I wasn't sure how she would react. There was a possibility that she wouldn't even believe me. Heck, I barely believed this myself.

Once my anger at Geraldine subsided, I expected a serious adrenaline crash from all this, and then reality would set in. I was no longer an only child.

Monday morning, I went into work, ready to ask Cassie if we could talk. She didn't typically come in until the afternoon, so I had plenty of time to stress before then.

"There you are," said Jeffrey, making a rare appearance at the front desk. "How far are you on the programming report?"

"I'm still working on it, but you'll have it Wednesday as requested."

His thin lips settled into a flat line as he shook his head. "I'm going to need it tomorrow."

"Tomorrow?"

"The meeting with the consultant has been moved up a day. I want time to review it so I'll need the report as soon as you can get it to me." He leaned his hands on the counter and a whiff of tobacco flooded my senses. On instinct, I rolled my chair backwards. "You know Pamela Abrams is retiring, right?"

Pamela was practically an institution in the library system and had been a staple at the main branch for longer than I'd been alive. Of course I'd heard about her retirement.

"Yes, but not for a few more weeks."

"They're holding interviews for her replacement on Thursday as well, and I said you'd sit in on them."

"Me?" This was quite a surprising development. "I've never taken part in the interview process before."

Jeffrey straightened. "They wanted someone low level used to working with the public, and you fit the description."

Low level. That'll make a girl feel important. "What time on Thursday and where?"

"At the main branch at ten a.m."

I opened the calendar on my computer and entered the information. "I'll be there."

With two taps on the counter, he said, "Get cracking on that report. The sooner I get it the better."

There were only a few hours left in my day, and I had softball practice tonight so I couldn't work over. I'd just have to take the files home and work into the night to get it done. "You'll have it in the morning," I assured him.

As he walked away, I scanned the library for Cassie. She'd been coming in around that time, but she wasn't at her regular table.

"Have you seen Cassie today?" I asked Miriam.

She looked up from her computer and blinked before looking in the same direction I had. "No, I haven't. She'll probably come in soon. Did you find some information for her?"

Did I ever. "I have a bit of a lead, yes."

"She'll be so excited. I tried to help her last week, but it's as if her mother never existed before Cassie was born." She tucked a pen behind her ear before reaching for a stack of books to her left. "I suggested that maybe her mother never actually lived in Pittsburgh, but Cassie is sure of it."

Curious, I said, "Do you remember her mother's name?"

Eyes lifted to the ceiling in thought, Miriam said, "Penbrook. Pendergrass. Something like that. Genevieve or Geraldine is the first name, I think."

"Not O'Malley?"

"No, she says her mother's ex-husband adopted her when she was young, but when they divorced, her mom took her maiden name back."

A plausible explanation. I wondered why Cassie was so convinced that her mother had lived in Pittsburgh. Geraldine had gone from Uniontown, an hour south of the city, straight to California as far as I knew. Or had she stayed in Pittsburgh for a while first? I'd only been seven so the time was a blur in my memory, and no doubt many details weren't shared with me at all. Maybe she'd worked here until she'd earned the money to get out west.

I wished I could remember where the few birthday cards had come from, but as a child, I wouldn't have understood postmarks. I just remember hearing about this distant place far, far away that could have been on another planet for all I knew. During the first few years after she left, there had been comments made that maybe someday I'd get to go visit her. Then the cards stopped coming, Dad stopped talking about her, and I did the same. We got so busy taking care of each other that she been relegated to this mysterious person who'd once lived with us.

Dad had been stressed in those early days. Even at a young age, I could tell that much. I never wanted to make things worse, and saying her name had been enough to change his mood. Not that he got angry or ever snapped at me. Just a shift to what I interpreted as sadness. I learned to keep my questions and my hopes to myself. By twelve or thirteen I'd given up on her ever coming back. That's probably when the anger started.

Anger that never went away.

For the rest of the afternoon, I worked on the report while keeping an eye out for Cassie. She never did come in, which had me worried. Last week she'd said she wasn't ready to give up, but what if she'd changed her mind? I had no idea how to find her. For all I knew, she was already back in California and Geraldine got her wish.

What would I do then? Was I supposed to go back to my life and forget that I had siblings who knew nothing about me? That didn't feel right, but I wasn't the only person affected by all this. Learning the truth would change their lives far more than mine. I knew the real Geraldine. The woman who willingly erased a child from her life. They had no idea.

With files stacked on my passenger seat, I headed to practice with a knot in my stomach. Between family revelations and trying to date again, my life was one giant ball of uncertainty, and I did not like it. What I wouldn't give to have my boring life back.

CHAPTER FOURTEEN

Never had softball felt less important in my life. As I carried my gear bag across the field, all I wanted to do was go home and hide.

My brain had raced throughout the drive to practice. A stream of endless questions. What would I tell Cassie? What would I tell Dad? Was this really the time to start dating? Even the programs at work didn't feel all that important anymore. Less than two weeks ago, I completely understood my life. I knew who my family was. I knew who *I* was.

Today, I knew none of those things.

"Hey there," said Dalton as I reached the bench. "Want to warm up?"

With little enthusiasm, I said, "Okay." We made our way onto the dirt, spreading out between third and home.

My mind was still elsewhere and I ended up throwing the ball over his head three times before deciding to put him out of his misery. "I'm not feeling great today. Why don't you find another warm-up partner?"

"No problem," he said, putting up no fight at all. Not that I blamed him.

I took a seat on the bench and stared at my toes. That's how Ryan found me.

"Are you okay?" he said.

Lifting my eyes, I tried to offer a smile in greeting but my heart wasn't in it. Since he knew at least part of what was going on, I didn't bother lying.

"Not really, no. Sorry about the other night. You should have woken me up."

He took a seat beside me. "I tried, but you were out."

"The allergy medicine does that. Sorry."

He bumped me with his shoulder. "Stop apologizing. You're good. I'm guessing that look on your face is because of the letter?"

Nodding, I tapped my glove against my thigh. "I don't know what to do."

"Who would? That was a big revelation. Did you see the girl today?"

"No, she never came in. What if she never does? I don't even know how to find her."

"You have an address for your mom. I'm guessing that isn't where you want to start, but it's something."

True. Would I go through Geraldine to reach these

siblings? I doubted she'd be much help considering her request.

I sighed. "I almost wish I'd never opened that letter."

Ryan squeezed my empty hand. "I know it feels like a lot right now, but some good can still come out of this. She might be happy to find you. I bet you'd be a really cool older sister."

What a crazy thought. "When I was little, I wanted a younger brother or sister. Who'd have believed that at thirty years old I'd get one of each?"

"Life can throw us curveballs like that." He rose off the bench and pulled me to my feet. "I'm always here to talk if you need me."

Before I could answer, a ball bounced off the bucket a couple of feet away. Wondering where it had come from, I looked around and found Fletcher standing near third base watching us with narrowed eyes.

Anger flaring, I said, "Did you throw that?"

Without answering, he sulked off toward first base at the same time that Coach Barry called for us to take the field.

"What is wrong with him?" I mumbled.

Ryan punched the center of his glove. "You know the answer to that. He's probably going to sulk for the rest of the season."

"Sulking is one thing, but that ball could have hit either one of us."

"I doubt he'd go that far. Come on, let's hit the field."

We jogged to our positions and I shot Fletcher a warning look before turning around to face the plate. I had enough to deal with this week. I did not need his childish antics added to the list. He didn't want to date me, but he didn't want me to date someone else. He wanted to be friends, but friends didn't go out of their way to make the other person feel like a schmuck.

"Be ready now," Coach said. "Here we go."

Infield practice went on for the next fifteen minutes, until we switched to batting practice. Coach Barry called Dalton in to hit first, and as we waited for him to come in from the outfield, I propped my glove on my hip and thought about what Ryan had said about me being an older sister. I'd been so focused on how to tell Cassie the truth, I hadn't thought about what would come next. Would she want a relationship with me? Would we spend time together? Get to know each other? There was so much unknown, but from the talk we'd had the week before, I felt confident that she'd want me in her life in some way.

I was still lost in the possibilities when I heard the smack of the bat against the ball, but my reflexes weren't quick enough to get my glove down in time. The line drive pegged off my right shin, and the pain was instantaneous. With a scream, I hit the ground, grabbing my leg —which felt like it had been shot. Rolling in pain, I closed my eyes and felt the sting of tears behind my eyelids.

Fletcher hit the dirt beside me. "Holy shit, Megan, are you okay?"

If I could speak, I'd have told him what a stupid question that was.

"Get her some ice," I heard Coach say. "Megan, I need you to breathe." That felt like too much to ask at the moment. Someone lifted my shoulders and propped me against them so that I was half sitting up. "Let me see," Coach said, trying to pry my hand loose. "Come on now. Let me have a look."

I wasn't trying to keep him from seeing the injury. I just couldn't unclench my hand. Nor could I take a full breath.

"I can't," I managed to whisper. "Oh my God, it hurts."

"In through your nose," said a voice in my ear, and I realized Ryan was the one behind me. "You can do it, Megan. We'll do it together. In through your nose." Focusing on his voice, I managed to let go of my leg while taking in air. "That's good," he said. "Now blow it out."

Coach straightened my leg and I managed to open my eyes. "Is it broken?" I asked in a shaky voice.

"I don't think so, but we definitely need to get ice on it." Snapping his fingers, he said, "Let's get her off the ground."

Ryan shifted and the next thing I knew I was being carried off the field. Coach kept hold of my leg and as soon as they set me down on the bench, Roxanne set a towel full of ice gently on my shin.

"Is that okay?" she said.

I nodded, since speaking was still difficult.

Coach sat down and draped my leg over his thigh. "I'm guessing a bone bruise," he said, lifting the ice and delicately testing the skin, which was quickly turning purple. "The ice will keep the swelling down, but there isn't much else you can do for this type of injury."

A bone bruise? I'd never even heard of that before. "Will I be able to play on Friday?"

"That's hard to tell. You need to wait and see how deep the bruising will go."

I leaned back against the dugout wall while pain vibrated up my leg. Just freaking great. Because I needed one more thing to go wrong right now.

"Everyone back on the field," he said, rising to his feet and carefully lowering my leg onto the bench. "If you can't bend the ankle without pain when it's time to go, we'll have someone get you home."

I hadn't even thought about driving. I wasn't about to leave my car here overnight, so I'd just have to suck it up and deal. As the team returned to practice, I closed my eyes and tried to focus on anything but the pain.

"I'm really sorry," said a deep voice.

Opening my eyes, I found Dalton hovering over me, brows drawn together and a look of true concern in his eyes.

"This isn't your fault. I should have been paying attention."

"I'm the one who hit the ball."

"And I'm the one who didn't react fast enough. Really, Dalton, you don't need to apologize."

He didn't look convinced. "If you need anything, just let me know. I'll get you more ice or drive you home. Whatever you need."

I appreciated the offer, though I had no intention of taking him up on any of it. "I'll keep that in mind, thanks."

As Dalton walked off, bat in hand, I leaned forward and lifted the ice. Purple and yellow now. Lovely.

Just freaking lovely.

———

PRACTICE CONTINUED as I sat on the bench, lamenting my idiot ways and wondering how my life had strayed so far from the norm. Where did my quiet, uneventful days go? And how did I get them back? As if Mother Nature decided to match my mood, the skies turned gray and thunder rolled in the distance. The threat was far enough off for practice to continue, but everyone kept an eye out for the first sign of lightning.

Wallowing in self-pity, I was surprised when a pooch rounded the corner of the dugout and hopped into my lap. I caught her weight on my stomach and quickly grabbed hold to make sure the animal didn't bounce onto my injured leg.

With big black eyes and a lulling tongue, she was white and strong and had a dark patch around her right eye. I assumed the *she* part based on the pink collar with a bow on it. Her owner followed seconds later. A woman not much taller than I was, with long curly hair, glasses, and a friendly smile. I assumed she was the significant other to one of my fellow players.

"I'm so sorry. She's usually better behaved than this." The woman lifted the dog's front legs back to the ground. Spotting my ice pack, she said, "Are you okay? Did she hurt you?"

"Oh, no. She didn't hit my leg." Scratching behind the dog's ear, I asked, "What's her name."

The stranger sat down. "This is Wendy, though I'm convinced he should have named her Chaos."

Wendy? Ryan's Wendy? But then who was the woman at the other end of the leash?

"She's cute," I said. "Boxer?"

She rolled her eyes. "Through and through. Goofy, clumsy, and a farting machine." As if remembering her manners, she said, "I'm Rachel, by the way. Ryan's sister."

His sister. My gut unclenched at the news. "Nice to meet you. I'm Megan."

Blue eyes went wide. "You're *the* Megan?"

I was pretty sure there were many more famous Megans than I. "Maybe?" I said. "I am friends with your brother, if that's *the* Megan you mean."

"Oh my gosh. I've heard so much about you. You're the reason I'm here."

"Me?"

"He wanted me to come meet you."

That seemed like a big move after only one date. "You came all the way from Akron to meet me?"

She laughed and the glasses slid down her nose. "No, I was already coming to town for the week, but he wanted me to come by the practice to meet you while I'm here. I know you haven't been going out for long so don't let this scare you." Cutting a quick glance her brother's way, she added, "He just really likes you, and he said we have a lot in common."

She had no idea how much. "You just finished college, right?"

"My master's, yeah. That's why I'm in town."

Before I could ask another question, thunder rocked the dugout and seconds later, a bolt of lightning cut across the clouds.

"Everybody off the field!" yelled Coach Barry as Wendy tried to crawl into Rachel's lap.

"You're okay, girl." To me the young woman said, "She's scared to death of loud noises."

As the team gathered and equipment was hurriedly

packed away, Ryan joined us in the dugout. Wendy squirmed with excitement, bending in half until her nubby little tail nearly touched her nose.

"Hey, girl. I'm happy to see you, too. How's your leg?" he asked me.

"Not thumping as much as it was." I moved the wet towel onto the bench and set both feet on the ground. "I need to pack up."

"I'll get it." Before I could stop him, Ryan bolted off to get my bag. Moments later, he had all my equipment inside, the bag zipped shut and leaning against the bench beside me. "Let me get my stuff together, and then we'll get you to your car."

"Ryan, I'm fine."

He looked down at the bruise spreading up my shin. "That doesn't look fine to me."

Determined, I flexed my ankle up and down. Pain shot along the top of my foot, but I managed to swallow the whimper. "See? Everything works."

"You should probably know now that he's the protective type," Rachel said, earning a hard glare from her brother. "What? It's true."

Thunder roared again, and Wendy howled her displeasure before cowering beneath the bench.

"We need to get her out of here," Ryan said.

"I'll take her to the car and wait for you there. Maybe I can turn on some music to calm her down." Rachel got to her feet at the same time heavy raindrops started dotting the dirt. "Come on, girl. We've gotta make a run for it."

Though I'd said I was fine, I was not looking forward to running through a rain shower on my injured leg. Walking was one thing. The force of my foot hitting the ground at a full run was something else. This was going to hurt like hell.

Ryan tossed his glove into his bag, and then threw mine and his over his shoulders. "You ready?"

I was going to have to be. Rising, I put my weight on my right foot and gasped from the pain. Clutching his arm, I balanced on one leg, waiting for the stars to clear. The rain grew heavier and I took a deep breath as I tried again. This time the ache was manageable so I nodded.

"Let's go."

We left the dugout at a run, and within ten feet I had to stop. I'd just have to walk. I was already wet so what was the difference now?

"You go on," I said, reaching for him to give me my bag. "There's no reason we both have to get soaked."

Shaking his head, Ryan ignored my order. "Not a chance."

Without warning, he swept me off my feet—literally—and started running once again.

"What are you doing?" I yelled, holding the ball cap on my head with one hand while clinging to his neck with the other.

He didn't answer, which I supposed was fair considering this feat was likely taking all the air he had. I may have been short but that didn't mean I was light.

"Give me the bags," Dalton said, coming from the parking lot to offer assistance.

Ryan slowed to a jog and the two men managed the handoff without the need to put me on my feet. Any woman who entertained the damsel in distress fantasy had no idea how humiliating the reality really was. I'd have fought harder to end the embarrassment, but we were almost to my car, and the memory of how badly it had hurt to run on my own was still fresh in my mind.

"Where are your keys?" Ryan asked, out of breath as we approached my Civic.

"In the front pocket of my gear bag," I answered.

"Front pocket!" he yelled to Dalton, who had the keys in hand and my doors unlocked seconds later. In true hero fashion, Ryan lowered me into the driver's seat as Dalton tossed my equipment on the back seat.

"You're sure you can drive?" he asked.

Nodding, I said, "Just go. You're already drenched."

To my surprise, he pressed a kiss to my forehead before closing the door and darting off. Dalton had disappeared—I feared *with* my keys—but they were hanging in the ignition. When had he managed that? The engine hummed to life and I cranked the heater as my teeth chattered. Water ran down my spine and my clothes felt heavy. Letting the car warm up, I pressed the gas pedal and was relieved to find the move only mildly painful.

With luck, this storm would blow over by the time I got home, but then taking my time getting into the apartment wouldn't make a difference now. I couldn't have gotten any wetter than I already was.

CHAPTER FIFTEEN

BY WEDNESDAY AFTERNOON, CASSIE HAD NOT RETURNED to the library. I was starting to lose hope that she ever would. Part of me said this was for the best. Neither of our lives would be turned upside down if I never saw her again. I would go back to being the only child I'd always believed myself to be, and Cassie would never know the person her mother truly was.

But another part—a much louder one—said there was no way I could forget what I'd learned. How could I go on with my life knowing these two people shared half of my DNA, and yet, I would never meet them? And how far would I go to find them? If I did contact Geraldine, as Ryan had suggested, I had no doubt she'd run interference in any way necessary in order to keep her secret. To keep *me* a secret.

Over the years, I'd come to terms with the idea that

Geraldine had simply not been cut out for motherhood. I could never forgive her, but I'd stopped taking her leaving personally. I'd convinced myself that she'd have left any child. But now I knew better. She'd mothered two other children. She never left them. *She only left me.*

That thought ripped open a wound that I'd tried really hard to cover up.

"Why didn't you tell me?" Miriam said, rolling my way and shoving me hard enough to send my chair careening away from the desk. "Thomas said you're seeing a guy on your team? Is it the one? Is it the cute guy that Fletcher tried to keep away from you?"

I pressed my feet to the floor to stop the chair and cringed when pain shot up my leg. The injury had turned into an almost perfectly round, purple circle a couple inches above my ankle. Though I could walk—be it with a slight limp—running was still not an option. I planned to attend practice, but it killed me that I wouldn't be able to play in the first game on Friday. Not with my lack of mobility at the moment.

"First off, Ryan and I have only been on one date, which didn't exactly go well. And how does Thomas even know about us?"

Miriam crossed her arms, a look of deep hurt in her eyes. "How could you not tell me?"

I'd never intended to keep her in the dark. "Between that report for Jeffrey and some other stuff going on in my life, I've just been a bit distracted. I'm sorry you found out from Thomas." Though I still wanted to know where he got the info. No doubt the gossip came from Fletcher. "Yes, it's the same guy, and we aren't at the seeing each other stage. It's been one date and he hasn't asked me for a second one."

That fact had hit me the night before when I found myself watching my phone, hoping he would send a text. I considered sending one first, but so far he'd seen me swell up like a blowfish thanks to a crustacean, and take a ball to the shin due to my wandering brain. Yes, he'd been chivalrous at the end of practice—and that kiss on the forehead felt encouraging—but he could also be second-guessing taking a chance on someone who was clearly a high-maintenance woman.

"Where did you go?" Miriam asked. "Was it romantic?"

It should have been. "We went out for Italian, but I messed up and ate a shrimp-stuffed appetizer."

Dark eyes went wide. "Oh, no."

"Oh, yes," I said, nodding my head. "Cue the swelling, the life-or-death emergency, and a scene that provided everyone in the restaurant an interesting story to share at their next dinner party."

"Megan, are you okay?"

"Yes. I'm here, after all. Ryan knew how to administer the injector, then he took me home and we hung out at my place until the allergy meds knocked me out."

Hurt turning to sympathy, she said, "I'm so sorry. Do you think that's why he hasn't asked you out again?"

I'd given this question a good bit of thought. "I don't know. It's only been five days, and he was really sweet at practice on Monday. Maybe we'll go out again." I hoped so, anyway.

Before Miriam could ask any more questions, my desk phone rang. The call was from Jeffrey's office. I hadn't seen him since turning in my report the morning before.

"Yes, sir?" I said after answering.

"I've forwarded you the email about the interviews tomorrow," he said, skipping a greeting. "The resumes are attached. You need to review them and make notes on which candidates might be the best fit."

I checked my inbox and found his email at the top. "I can do that." Opening the message, I scanned the attachments listed at the bottom to make sure they all came through. They were titled with the name of each applicant, and when I reached the third one down, my heart stopped.

Rachel Stallings.

"I'm going straight to the meeting in the morning," Jeffrey said, though I was barely listening now. "I'm not sure how long this consultant business will take. If we go into the afternoon, I won't be in at all."

"Okay," I said, still staring at the name on my screen.

Without waiting for him to say more, I hung up the phone and dropped my forehead onto the desktop.

"What is it?" Miriam said. "What did he say?"

"Shoot me, Miriam. Put me out of my misery."

"You're scaring me, Megan. What happened? Have they already decided what programs to cut?"

If only that was the issue.

Lifting my head and turning her way, I asked, "Have you ever started a relationship with a lie?"

Brows drawn, she said "What are you talking about?"

"I told Ryan that I work in a bookstore because I didn't want him to think I was an uptight, boring librarian. Now his sister is one of the interview candidates. She's going to find out that I *don't* work at a bookstore, which means I have to tell him the truth before tomorrow."

"Megan, why would you lie about what you do?"

"I don't know!" I said, throwing my hands in the air. "I was still stinging from the breakup with Fletcher and how he never thought I was exciting enough or interesting enough or whatever enough. This guy was cute and talkative and I wanted to keep him talking." My voice faded to a near whisper. "I thought that once I got him to like me, it would be safe to tell him the truth."

Pointing out the obvious, she said, "That doesn't sound like a very good plan."

"I know." With a whimper, I dropped my head back to

the desk. "I've tried to tell him a couple of times, but something always gets in the way."

Miriam patted me on the back. "Maybe it'll be okay. Maybe if you explain it just like that, he'll be flattered that you liked him enough to lie?"

We both knew that was not going to happen. Lifting my head, I stared at Rachel's name on my screen. "He's such a sweet guy."

"There will be other sweet guys," Miriam assured me. "I can see if Devon has any single friends."

Just because a quasi-blind date had worked for Becca did not mean I was ready to go there. "Thanks, but I'll pass."

The pity in her eyes was almost too much to bear. "Okay, hon. But if you change your mind, say the word and I've got you."

"I appreciate that." And I did. Though I would not be changing my mind. If anything, I should probably spare others from the drama my life had suddenly become. If I could, I'd spare myself as well, but that didn't look possible anytime soon.

———

I showed up at practice with one mission, and though I was nauseous with dread, I would not let Ryan leave this field without knowing exactly what I did for a living.

"What are you doing here?" Theresa asked as I hobbled my way to the bench.

"Why wouldn't I be here?"

She pointed at my leg. "Because you can't play on that leg."

A temporary condition. "For now."

"What are you doing here?" asked Coach Barry as we reached the dugout.

Really? Had *everyone* expected me not to show?

"Am I not on this team?" I asked, struggling to control my annoyance.

"Yeah, but you can't play," he pointed out.

"I can't play *right now*, but I'm not out for the season. And I can still get some batting practice."

Satisfied with my answer, Coach said, "I appreciate the dedication." Over my head, he yelled, "Let's get ready to take the field. Brower, you're at second for Knox, and Leroux cover short for Stallings."

"Wait," I said. "Cover for Stallings? Is Ryan not coming?"

"He called me about an hour ago," he replied, carrying the five-gallon bucket of balls to home plate. I limped along behind him. "Something about a big meeting tomorrow so he's working late."

What the heck? How was I going to tell him now? The only reason I hadn't done it the night before was because this didn't feel like something one should confess over the phone. And definitely not through a text.

But a call tonight would be better than him finding out from Rachel tomorrow.

Now I had a half hour to sit on the bench and stress instead of being on the field where I'd at least feel like I belonged here. Time sitting meant time to think. Time to question. Why had I lied about my job? I couldn't keep blaming Fletcher. This was about me. What was wrong with me? What was wrong with being a librarian? With liking books and foreign films and staying home on a Saturday night?

Nothing. Nothing at all. Yet I'd gotten some idea in my head that I could only be interesting to a guy if I was someone else. What an idiotic notion. I didn't want my boring life? Wish granted. How about a letter from your mother and a couple new siblings and a boomerang ex and a detached boss and a budding romance kicked off with a lie and a near-death experience.

Talk about karma. I deserved every bit of it.

While I simmered about the pickle my life had become, practice progressed but ended early. Within an hour we were all headed back to our cars, and because the universe wasn't done with me just yet, Fletcher caught me at my car.

"Can we talk?"

Anxious to get home and call Ryan, I opened my car door. "Not today, Fletcher."

"Megan, please."

I'd never heard that tone in his voice before. "What is

it?" I said, leaning on my car. Batting had been more painful than I'd expected, and all this walking wasn't helping either.

Fletcher looked around while running a hand through his hair. "I didn't want to do this here."

My gut tightened. "Do what?"

"Can we go get a drink or something?"

I had something else to do. "This isn't a good day. Can it wait?"

Shifting from one foot to the other, he said, "Just give me half an hour. Don't I deserve that much?"

Did he really want me to answer that? "Fletcher, I'm having a really crappy week, and as far as I can tell, it's going to get even worse very soon. So if you need to say something, just say it so I can go home."

"Fine. I never should have broken up with you."

For heaven's sake. "What are you talking about?"

He shook his head. "I was wrong. I was an idiot."

On that we could agree. "Is this because I went out with Ryan?"

His eyes locked with mine. "You went out with Ryan?"

So maybe he hadn't been the one to tell Thomas. "Yes, I did."

"Come on, Meg. You can do better than that guy."

Said the man who dumped me. "Whether *that guy* or someone else, who I go out with is my business. Where is all this coming from? You had no problem saying we were through, *and* you have a girlfriend. One you seem to keep forgetting when we have these conversations."

Fletcher crossed his arms. "Fiona and I aren't working out."

Oh, now this was making sense. "So you're afraid you're about to be single, and we can't have that."

"What's that supposed to mean?"

"You started seeing me less than two weeks after breaking up with… what was her name?" I had to think for a second. "Hayley, right? The first time I was in your apartment half of her things were still there. You told me they belonged to your sister."

"What does that—"

"You can't stand to be alone," I said, cutting him off. "Fletcher, do you like yourself at all?"

That got me a blank stare. "What?"

"I mean, you're a good guy. A bit needy, but you aren't a bad person. Why don't you try being single for a while. Figure out what you *actually* want instead of leaping into relationships just so you have someone around to give you attention twenty-four seven."

Clearly offended, he said "I can be alone."

"Can you?" I asked. "Really?" He remained silent, which didn't surprise me. "Look, I'm the last person who should be giving relationship advice or babbling some self-help BS, but neither one of us is going to find the right person until we like who we are first. I lost my entire identity when I was with you because I had no idea who I was to begin with. I still don't, but I know we aren't a match. And you know that, too. You weren't wrong eight months ago, Fletcher. We *are* two very different people. I don't know if that's the case with you and Fiona or not, but if that doesn't work out, you'll survive. You might even be better off spending a little time with yourself. There's a good, caring man in there somewhere. Under all the bluff and ego. You should take the time to get to know him. He's worth the effort."

He looked off into the distance for several seconds before meeting my gaze once again. The vulnerability in his eyes made me want to hug him.

"You really mean all that?"

I offered a heartfelt smile. "I do." Funny that I'd once imagined saying those two little words to this man in a very different context. "You've got potential, Fletcher. You're going to make some lucky girl really happy one day. But I'm not that girl."

Expression softening, his lips turned up in a half grin. "Potential, huh?"

"Yeah."

He slowly backed away. "I guess I'll see you Friday."

"I'll be cheering from the bench, but I'll be there."

With a silent nod, he turned and walk across the now empty parking lot to the obnoxiously bright-red muscle car that was the perfect representation of the man who owned it. And I slid into my nondescript, practical little car feeling as if I'd accomplished something. It was time to take my own advice, and the first step was to clear things up with Ryan. Whether that went well or not, I too would survive. That was a handy thing to know.

I NO LONGER FELT NAUSEOUS about making the call. Nervous, but not nauseous. I guess I had Fletcher to thank for that. Everything I'd said to him applied to me as well. Heaven knew I wasn't perfect, but I liked to think that I had potential, too. We were all a work in progress, after all.

Sitting on my couch, I dialed Ryan's number. I hadn't spoken to him on the phone before. We'd only exchanged texts so far. This wasn't the way I wanted to do this, but I was going to feel so much lighter once he knew. No matter how he reacted, the truth would be out and we could either move forward or stop here. I would deal either way.

He picked up on the second ring and my courage wavered when his tone was slightly less than friendly.

"Hey, I can't talk."

"I'm sorry. I thought you'd be off work by now."

"No, I'm still here."

"Oh." The nausea returned with a vengeance. "I'll let you go then."

I was about to ask if he could call me later when he said, "I'll see you Friday."

The line went dead and I sat blinking, phone still pressed to my ear. Maybe he was having a bad day. Or was stressed about the meeting Coach had mentioned. I shouldn't have taken his abrupt tone personally, but I couldn't help but feel… scolded. Like I'd crossed some line I shouldn't have.

The only option left was to talk to Rachel after the interview. To explain my faulty thinking and hopefully convince her to let me tell Ryan before she did. Or she might say her brother deserved better and that would be it. That was no less than I deserved, after all, but in the grand scheme of things, this wasn't the worst lie in the world. I hadn't catfished him or pretended to be someone I'm not. He knew my name and where I lived and even knew the details about Cassie, which not even Dad knew.

If the roles were reversed, I'd like to think I'd be forgiving, but would I? Could I continue seeing a guy who didn't tell me the truth from the start? How could I trust him after that? I couldn't, and that realization put the situation into perspective. A lie was a lie. I would not be asking for forgiveness or expecting another date. The best I could hope for was a cleared conscience and a lesson learned.

CHAPTER SIXTEEN

I HAD NEVER GIVEN MYSELF SO MANY PEP TALKS IN MY life. From my first cup of tea to the moment I walked through the ornate black doors into the main library, one simple phrase kept running through my mind.

You can do this.

This was by far my favorite of all the branches. The first in the system, housed in its original building dedicated in 1895, the main branch was expansive, ornate, and included a music hall and a museum. Numerous large windows let in a ton of natural light, while the columns and arches, visible in every direction, hearkened back to another time. The only reason I'd never requested a transfer to this location was because I had no desire to live in Oakland, which was one of the busier parts of the city thanks to being the home of the University of Pittsburgh.

I also didn't want to be so far from my friends, and commuting would be a bear.

Stepping up to the long front desk, I found a familiar face. "Morning, Donald. How are you?"

"I'm good, Megan. What brings you all the way out here?"

"I'm sitting in on some interviews this morning. The email didn't tell me where they were holding them. Do you know?"

He pushed up his glasses as sunlight glistened off his almost bald head. "Third floor conference room. You know where the elevator is, right?"

"I do, thanks."

I made my way through the quiet space, passing beneath the arches on my way to the far back corner where the elevators were. For a second I considered taking the stairs, but I'd worn a dressier pair of shoes that were not broken in and didn't want to chance a blister. There was also the sore leg to consider.

Casting a quick glance toward the children's room as I went by, I made a note to stop by the space after the interviews. Though we didn't have a designated kid's area due to lack of space, I still liked to get ideas for small touches we could add where possible.

As I approached the elevator, I heard someone call my name and turned to find Pamela walking my way.

"Hello, there," I said.

"Hello, yourself. What brings you to my neck of the

woods today?"

Her once bright-red curls were now dark gray, but little else had changed. She had an interesting face with a sloped nose, full brows, and a tiny mole right above her top lip. One of my favorite fellow librarians, Pamela was sharp as a whip, and I wished we weren't losing her to retirement.

"Didn't they tell you? I'm sitting in on the interviews to replace you." I'd assumed she'd be included as well, since she knew the job better than anyone.

She smacked her forehead. "That's today? I completely forgot with this consultant thing they've thrown me into."

My ears perked up. "You're in on the consultant meeting?"

"Yes, but not willingly. You'd think having one foot out the door would get me out of boring money stuff, but I guess not."

I would have killed to be in her shoes, and not because I wanted early retirement. "Do you know anything about the consultant and what he might suggest for cuts?"

Pamela pursed her lips, revealing more wrinkles than I'd noticed before. "I've met him, and I don't know that he's coming in with any preconceived ideas. That's what the meeting is for, after all. For the branch managers to give their input, and then he'll take the suggestions and crunch the numbers, I guess."

Then I just needed Jeffrey to make the right suggestions. Something I didn't trust him to do. I couldn't put my finger on anything specific, but I had a bad feeling about the fate of my programs being in his hands.

Before I could ask another question, Pamela said, "Here's the consultant now if you want to meet him." I spun to find a very familiar face staring back at me. As my heart skidded to a stop, she introduced us. "Megan Knox, this is Ryan Stallings."

"Ryan?" I said.

"Megan?" Dark brows drew together. "What are you doing here?"

"You've met?" Pamela said.

Jaw tight, I held his gaze. "Yes, we've met."

Though I should have been trying to explain myself, I couldn't get past the fact that *he* was the consultant. He'd said he helped people manage their money, and I supposed in some twisted way that was an accurate statement. But I couldn't help but feel like I'd been purposely misled.

"I guess it makes sense to run into you at a library," he said, and I realized he had yet to catch on.

"That is where librarians are usually found," Pamela said with a chuckle.

Seconds passed as the truth clicked into place, and I watched his expression change. "Wait. I thought you worked in a bookstore."

I embraced my right to remain silent, since I had no

excuse for the outright lie. Poor Pamela was very confused.

"A library and a bookstore are similar, I guess." Her eyes went from Ryan's face to mine. "I feel like I've walked into a conversation already in progress so I'm going to leave now and let you two carry this on alone."

Neither of us stopped her as she walked away.

"So you're a librarian?" Ryan said.

"Yes."

"But you told me you work in a bookstore?"

"Yes."

He crossed his arms. "I'm going to need a little more than one-word answers."

"You told me you work in finance," I reminded him.

"And I do."

"Helping people cobble together a retirement plan, and working with a major institution to decide where money is and isn't worth spending are two very different things."

A muscle twitched along his jaw. "Explaining what I do is complicated."

"So you didn't think I was smart enough to understand the word *consultant*?"

"At least I didn't tell an outright lie. Why didn't you just say you were a librarian?"

Why didn't I? Oh, right. Because I'm an idiot. "Some people make negative assumptions about librarians, and I wanted you to get to know me first."

"I wouldn't have made those assumptions."

Anger waning, I looked away. "I know that now. I've been trying to tell you the truth since the night of our date, but the timing never worked out."

"Stallings, what's the hold up?" boomed Jeffrey, far too loudly for the library floor. "Ms. Knox, why aren't you in the interviews? Do you two know each other?"

Ryan shook his head. "I thought we did, but I was wrong."

The words sliced like a knife, and I regretted every word I'd just uttered. The finality in his statement said it all. I'd messed up. I'd lied. And I hadn't even had the dignity to apologize.

He and Jeffrey walked away, leaving me frozen in place. How had I made such a mess of everything?

"Megan?" said a voice from my left. "They called down looking for you," Donald said. "Are you okay?"

No, I wasn't. "I'm sorry," I said. "Tell them I'm on my way."

"You sure? You look a little pale."

Taking a deep breath, I nodded and offered an empty smile. "I'm fine. I just got a little sidetracked." He didn't look convinced so I tried the smile again before giving up and crossing the short distance to the elevator. The world went on and I had a job to do. I just hoped I would keep it together until I could get to my car and have a really good cry.

———

PAYING attention hadn't been easy over the next hour. Concerns warred in my mind from what would happen to the programs to *if* Ryan would ever speak to me again. I wouldn't blame him if he didn't, but we still had to play on the team together. We weren't likely to be friends, but I hadn't exactly committed the crime of the century. As far as sins went, I wanted to think I was still redeemable. Even if only to the point that we could be civil to each other on the field.

Rachel was the last interview, because heaven forbid the universe cut me a break and let me get the final blow over with quickly. We were total strangers except for a one-minute conversation a few nights before so this wasn't the same as the scene with Ryan, but she had looked quite confused when she took a seat and found me among the interviewers.

Because Pamela did so much, we were actually hiring two people to take her place. One required more experience, but a newbie fresh out of school could fill the other. That's where Rachel came in. She was up against only one other applicant, and even if I'd never met her before, I'd have given her my vote for the position. She was smart, had done a great deal of work while in college, and possessed excellent people skills, which were needed in a job that required constant interaction with the public.

When the interview ended, I gave an excuse and hurried from the room, hoping to catch her.

"Rachel," I called as she pressed the button for the elevator. "Can I talk to you?"

To my surprise, she offered a genuine smile. "Sure. I was surprised to see you in there."

"Yeah. About that…" I looked around for a place we might find some privacy. Pointing to a table at the edge of the genealogy section, I said, "Can we sit down?"

She agreed and we both took a seat.

"In case you don't know," Rachel began, "Ryan is downstairs."

Oh, I knew all right. "We ran into each other. That went… not well."

"I'm not surprised. My brother can be a stickler for the truth. I'm guessing you don't work in a bookstore *and* here at the library?"

"Technically, I work at another branch, but no, I don't work in a bookstore at all." Hoping she might understand, I said, "You see, sometimes when I tell people that I'm a librarian, they make a few assumptions."

Rachel snorted. "Tell me about it. I've lost track of how many guys have made a lewd joke about me letting my hair down and turning into some wild cat in bed."

"Yes," I said. Though that wasn't exactly the reaction I got. "Except for me, it goes the other way. They think I must be boring and never take my nose out of a book."

The leggy blond looked perplexed. "I haven't gotten

that one." Of course, she hadn't. She was young and beautiful and not the size of a Cabbage Patch doll. "But I get it," she added. "Ryan should, too. He has the same hang-up."

Now she'd lost me. "What do you mean?"

"Did he tell you he's a consultant?"

"No, he didn't. I had no idea until we met by accident today."

Lips pursed, Rachel rolled her eyes. "He's gotten crap from people who think consultant equates to con artist. You can imagine not everyone is happy to have an outsider come in and tell them what to change. Some of the jobs he's taken have resulted in everything from his car getting keyed to someone putting salt in his coffee."

That was much more than I had to deal with.

"But he didn't know that I was involved with the library or had any connection to his job. Why not tell me the truth?"

Rachel crossed her arms on the table. "Sadly, it doesn't just happen at work. Some woman he dated in Chicago broke up with him because she was too embarrassed to tell her friends she was dating a consultant. That's only one person, but those things can stick with you."

Yes, they could. "So we basically did the same thing for similar reasons. I'd laugh at the irony if I could get that look on his face out of my head."

"He isn't unreasonable," she said. "Once he gets over

the initial anger, he'll normally hear a person out." Her phone buzzed and she checked the screen. "Speak of the devil. Ryan says his meeting is over. If you want, we can go down together. Maybe with two against one we can convince him to at least let you explain."

"You'd do that for me?"

She slid the phone back into her purse. "Ryan hasn't talked about anyone like he's talked about you. I know you guys still barely know each other, but he's pretty guarded about who he spends his time with. So long as you haven't lied about anything else…"

"No," I said. "Nothing. He's been to my house. He knows my family history. Heck, he's even seen me without makeup on. There's no hiding anything there."

Her laughter filled the space before she remembered where we were. In a whisper, she said, "I'm meeting him in the coffee shop. Let's go straighten this out."

"I would love to." As I pushed my chair in, I caught sight of another familiar face across the room. Why hadn't I thought of this? Of course, she'd be in the genealogy department with the largest amount of archives in the city. "Wait," I said to Rachel. "I need to talk to someone first."

Rachel followed by gaze. "Oh, okay, but Ryan is waiting."

I couldn't let Cassie slip through my fingers again. "You go on down. I'll be there in a couple minutes."

"Should I tell him you're coming?" she asked as I made my way through the tables.

"Yes." Trying to run the two scenarios through my mind at the same time, I stopped and spun to face her. "No. Just keep him there. I'll be there as soon as I deal with this."

If Ryan was still angry, he would either leave to avoid me or get mad at Rachel for taking my side. All I had to do was convince Cassie to meet me for dinner tonight, and then I could hurry downstairs.

When I turned back around, the seat where Cassie had been was empty. How could she have moved that quickly? I scanned the area and was about to ask another patron if they saw where she'd gone when her head popped up from behind a shelf. I hurried through the tables to reach her.

"Cassie," I said as she began to walk off in the other direction. "Cassie, wait." As if not sure if she'd heard her name or not, she paused and tilted her head. "Cassie, over here."

She took a step back, searching for the voice and when our eyes met, hers went wide. "Hey, Megan. What are you doing here?"

After dodging a slow-moving patron to reach her, I took a second to catch my breath. "I was sitting in on some interviews and they just wrapped up. I was surprised when you stopped coming to the library."

"Oh, Thomas told me about this collection, so I've been working here for the last few days."

Thomas. Why hadn't I thought to ask him if he'd seen her? "Have you found anything?"

Her face fell. "Not yet. Based on my DNA results, I have a lead on someone who might be a distant uncle. I've reached out but no response yet, so I'm back to searching old birth records."

Hearing the seconds tick away in my head, I searched for a way to ask her to meet me without sounding creepy or cryptic.

"I think I might know something about your mom, but I don't have time to discuss it right now. Could we meet later? Maybe grab a bite?"

"Did you find something?" Cassie said, ignoring the invite to dinner.

"Kind of." I had no idea how long Rachel could keep Ryan in the building. "Where are you staying? Maybe we can meet close to there."

"I'm at a short-term rental on the South Side. Are you saying you have information about my mom? What is it?"

"I'm sorry. I really have to go. Meet me at Café Du Jour at six o'clock, okay? It's on East Carson Street. You can't miss it."

"But, Megan…"

Rushing off, I said, "I'll see you there at six o'clock. I'll tell you everything then."

Skipping the elevator, I charged down the stairs,

anxious to reach the coffee shop as soon as possible. By the time I hit the bottom step, my injured leg was on fire, and I had the start of a mean blister on my left heel. Hobbling as best I could, I entered the little shop out of breath, but Rachel and Ryan weren't there. I returned to the main space and looked in all directions, thinking maybe they were waiting in another area.

They were nowhere in sight, and my leg and heel hurt too badly to search the entire library. As I bent down to pull my foot out of the shoe then bend the back under, Donald found me once again.

"There you are. Someone named Rachel said to tell you she tried but she's sorry. Do you know what that means?"

With a sigh, I pushed my hair out of my face and wiped my damp forehead. "I do, thanks." He waited as if hoping I would explain. I would not be doing that. "I need to get back to work. Have a good afternoon, Donald."

"You, too," he said as I limped toward the exit with as much dignity as I could muster.

I needed an adhesive bandage, a change of shoes, and a stiff drink. None of which I had with me. That's when I made the executive decision that I deserved the rest of the day off. I couldn't remember the last time I'd used vacation time, and if there was ever a day I'd earned some, this was that day.

CHAPTER SEVENTEEN

BY THE TIME I WALKED INTO MY APARTMENT, I'D MADE another important decision. I couldn't possibly talk to Cassie without talking to Dad first. I'd been an idiot for not telling him right away. We'd always been a team. The two of us against the world. How could I have possibly even considered doing this without him?

I'd had lots of *bad* ideas lately. Telling lies. Keeping secrets. Running down three flights of stairs in brand-new shoes.

Stretched out on my couch with a bag of frozen peas on my shin, I'd called Dad in the hopes he could meet me before my dinner with Cassie. He said he'd be home by five thirty. That didn't leave me a lot of time, but thankfully, his place was only minutes from Café Du Jour.

"Dad?" I called as I walked through the door of his house at exactly five thirty. To my surprise, a black cat

202

met me at the edge of the living room. "Who are you?" The feline meowed a response, but there was a clear language barrier. "Are you supposed to be here?"

"He is," Dad said, coming down the stairs. "This is Boris. He's Nessa's grandcat. I'm watching him for the next few days while her daughter and her family are out of town."

That begged the obvious question. "Why isn't Nessa watching him?"

"Her apartment building has strict rules against pet visitors." Tapping Boris on the head, Dad added, "He's a friendly guy. Doesn't move much, but he's a solid eater."

I could tell that from the size of him. He made Becca's full-grown cat look like a week-old kitten.

"He's very pretty." I'd have visited with the newcomer, but I didn't have time today. "Dad, I have something I need to show you."

"I have water on to boil so come into the kitchen. We can talk in there."

I followed him into the next room and as he went to the stove, I took a seat at the small mobile island and pulled the letter from my purse. "I got this a couple of weeks ago."

"What is it, honey?"

"You should just read it first."

Concern creased his brow as he unfolded the letter and read silently. I watched his face shift from curiosity to shock to anger.

"She had other children."

We'd obviously made the same assumption, that Geraldine never would have had more kids.

"I'm sorry I didn't bring this to you the minute I got it. I was going to tell you that day at Eat'n Park, but I didn't want to bring Geraldine up when you were finally moving on with Nessa."

"Megan, you don't have to protect me." His voice was more stern than usual. "Have you sent her a response?"

"No, I haven't done anything. Yet."

He crossed to the stove and turned off the burner. "I'd hoped that someday she might reach out to you, but not like this. I see she hasn't changed one bit."

"Have you been in touch with her at all over the years?"

"She sent me her address about fifteen years ago. I think she expected that if anything happened to me, you'd go live with her."

"Why didn't you tell me that?"

Dad tossed the letter onto the island. "If you'd have asked to find her, I'd have let you know where she was. I guess maybe I was selfish, but I didn't trust her not to hurt you all over again."

This recent letter showed he'd been right. The one time, after all these years, that she'd reached out hadn't been to apologize or reconnect. Just a request to help keep *me* a secret. Dad wasn't the selfish one. Geraldine was.

"The girl she's talking about has been coming into the library," I said. "I'm meeting her in less than thirty minutes."

"What are you going to tell her?"

The only thing I could tell her. "The truth. That we have the same mother. That Geraldine left when I was seven and never came back."

Leaning his elbows on the stainless-steel countertop, he said, "How do you think she's going to take it?"

That was the million-dollar question. "I have no idea."

"Do you want me to come with you?"

I'd considered that. "I think I need to go alone, but am I doing the right thing? She's told me she's determined to find out about her mother's past and her family, but I doubt this is what she expected to dig up. Letting her know we're sisters—which I'm still processing and I've had two weeks to think about it—is one thing. But I'm going to tell her that her mother walked away from another child. That's a heavy thing to learn."

Quiet for several seconds, Dad finally said, "It's heavy, but as you said, it's the truth. If that's what she's here for, then I'm not sure you have any other choice. With that kind of determination, she's bound to find out eventually, and she'd likely be more upset to know you *didn't* tell her when you had the chance."

I agreed. "That's my thinking. I guess I just needed to hear it from someone else."

"Are you sure you don't want me to come?" He checked the clock above the back door. "Where are you meeting her?"

"She's staying here on the South Side so I told her to meet me at Café Du Jour. And I do think I should go alone, but thank you for offering." Sliding off the bar stool, I shoved the letter back into my purse. "I'll let you know how it goes."

"Please, do." Walking me to the door, he threw his arm across my shoulders and gave me a squeeze. "I'm sorry you have to do this at all."

I knew he carried guilt about how things had gone with Geraldine. As if he'd picked the wrong person to have kids with, and I'd been the one to pay the price. He couldn't have known what she would do, and if he hadn't fallen for the beautiful girl in his history class, I wouldn't even be here.

"You know you're a great dad, right? I wouldn't trade my childhood with you for anything." I didn't tell him this often enough.

Dad pressed a kiss to my forehead. "And you're the best daughter a man could ever hope to have. One call and I'm there, okay?"

"Thank you."

Boris offered his own goodbye, or at least I assumed that's what he was saying. "Wish me luck, Boris. If only my life was as simple as yours." He offered the same meow in the same tone, yet I felt as if we'd made a connection.

After sending Dad a wave before reaching my car, I checked the time on my phone. I had just under ten minutes to travel the nearly twenty blocks down to the restaurant. My stomach was in knots, but talking with Dad had helped. One less secret weighing on my shoulders. Now to bring the biggest one into the light.

———

I ARRIVED a few minutes before six and took a seat away from the other diners, but not so far that Cassie couldn't see me from the entrance. Café Du Jour was a small, European-inspired restaurant that drew a smaller crowd, which felt like the right setting for the conversation to come. No loud music to talk over. No large groups disrupting the quiet ambiance. Not that there was a perfect setting to receive the news I had to deliver, but this particular eatery provided a calm vibe I hoped would help.

Cassie breezed in at exactly six, and without waiting for the hostess, rushed to my table and sat down. "Why did you rush off earlier? I'm dying to know what you've found out."

Fighting the butterflies in my stomach, I followed the plan I'd come up with in the last ten minutes. "First, let's make sure I have the right person. What is your mother's name?"

"Geri Pendleton. Well, Geraldine is her full name."

A part of me had wanted her to say a different name.

"Right. That's the name I have." I needed to take this slow. "The reason you haven't been able to find a record of her here is because she wasn't born in Pittsburgh."

Sitting up straighter, she shook her head. "But she's from Pittsburgh. That's the one thing I know for sure."

"Her hometown is close to here. About an hour southeast, actually. It's called Uniontown."

"I've never heard of that."

Which explained why she hadn't found anything. "It's where I was born, as well."

Cassie leaned forward. "Did you know her?"

"Yes, I did."

"Oh my gosh. This is crazy." She scooted to the edge of her seat. "How? I mean, you would have been a kid. Was she your babysitter or something?"

Jaw tight, I took a steadying breath. "She wasn't my babysitter, Cassie. She was my mother."

The waitress picked that exact moment to step up to the table. "Good evening, ladies. What can I get you to drink tonight?"

Cassie stared at me, stunned into silence, while I smiled at the waitress. "Could we have two glasses of water?"

"Sure thing. Do you need more time to look at the menu?"

"We're going to need several minutes, thanks."

The young brunette cast a glance from me to Cassie. "Got it. Take all the time you need."

As she walked away, I stayed quiet, giving Cassie the time she needed to absorb the shock. When she finally broke her silence, the words came out on a whisper.

"How?"

"Geraldine and my dad, James, went to school together. She got pregnant with me at the start of her senior year of high school, and they got married a week after graduation. I arrived a few days later."

Gripping the table, she stared at the tiny vase centerpiece. "I don't understand. You have to be talking about a different person."

"I'm not. Look, I know this is hard to hear."

She shook her head quickly from side to side. "If she's your mother, then why have I never heard of you? Did your dad take you away from her? Is that what happened? Does she even know where you are?"

This sucked as much as I'd feared. "When I was seven, she left. I never saw her again after that. I just knew she was in California, but I didn't know where exactly."

"What do you mean *she left*? She wouldn't just leave a child like that. My mother is a lot of things, but she isn't a monster."

"She was young," I said in her defense. Not that twenty-five was that young, or that her age justified her actions. "She said she didn't want that life. Being a mom and a wife in a small town just wasn't for her."

Pushing back, Cassie said, "No. No way. You were just a kid, right? That may be the story they told you, but that's all it is. A story. Mom would *never* have done something like that."

"I'm afraid she did. I was seven, Cassie. I remember the day she left like it happened yesterday. Dad tried to get her to stay, but she had her mind made up."

She leaned back in her chair, arms crossed and defiant. "I don't believe you. I don't believe any of this. If you think she has money and you'll get some, you're wasting your time. If you just get off on tricking people, then I don't know what to tell you, but I'm not falling for it."

"Cassie, I have nothing to gain by telling you this. Other than us getting to know each other, but that's up to you. You said you wanted to know about your mother's past no matter what you found. Well, this is her past. It's difficult to process. I only learned about you last weekend, and I'm still not sure how *I* feel. I mean, she *left* me but she *raised* you. Knowing that doesn't make me feel good."

"There's no way it went down like that," she said. "I'm sorry you were fed a bunch of lies, but I won't sit here and listen to them."

As she jumped to her feet, I pulled out the one piece of evidence she couldn't refute. "Just read this letter and you'll see."

"I'm not reading anything." She jerked her backpack onto her shoulder. "I'm out of here."

"But, Cassie—"

Before I could finish, she stormed out of the restaurant. Clenching the letter, I ran after her. "Wait, if you'll just..." The words trailed off as she melted into the shadows from the street lights and disappeared from view. "...read this," I muttered. With a deep sigh, I went back inside to get my things. After catching the waitress' eye and letting her know I was leaving, I stepped out into the cool night air, heart-heavy and bone-tired. I'd been prepared for shock and questions and maybe even tears. Not outright rejection.

Since I had no way to reach her and highly doubted Cassie would ever return to the library, this was it. My one brief encounter with the sister I never knew I had. Deep down, I'd wanted the same things she'd talked about. The reunion. The family gatherings. Getting to know her and this brother I also knew nothing about. None of that would happen now.

Fighting back tears, I headed for my car and remembered that Donna lived less than a block away. I could have gone back to Dad's place, but he'd want to fix things and right now I just needed a shoulder to cry on.

Making the short walk up Carson, I turned left on South 12th Street and could see her building straight ahead.

Minutes later, Donna answered my knock and the moment I saw her, I fell apart.

"Oh, sweetie," she said, wrapping an arm around my shoulders and pulling me inside.

———

"And then she stormed out," I said, finishing the story with a lap full of tissues. "I never should have told her."

Donna carried the garbage can over and set it at the end of the couch. "You had to tell her, Meg. Your mother has kept her secrets long enough. You don't owe her anything."

"But what was the point? Cassie doesn't believe me, and I'm sure she's going to tell Geraldine all about this crazy girl who thinks she's her daughter. I can only imagine the letter I'll get then."

"Screw her." Plopping down beside me, she rubbed my back. "If another letter shows up, then you ignore it. Like I said, you don't owe her anything. If she doesn't have the nerve to come over here and talk to you, then anything she has to say on paper can go in the trash."

Blowing out a deep breath, I tossed the pile of tissues into the can. "I wish I'd thrown the first one away. Then none of this would be happening."

"True, but as messed up as this is, you never know.

Cassie could come around and contact you someday." Pointing out the obvious, she added, "This is what happens when secrets stay buried. They fester and people get hurt. You're both better off this way."

I didn't feel better off, but she was right. Though I held little hope of ever hearing from Cassie again. Donna's phone dinged for the third time, and she ignored it as she had the other two.

"You can answer that," I said. "I didn't think to ask if you were busy before barging in here."

"Don't be crazy. I always have time for you," she said, checking her phone. "This is Becca. My exhibition venue fell through, and she's sending me links to other options."

Donna had been working on her collection of photographs documenting racial justice activism and diversity in the city for the last five years. She finally felt confident enough to launch the show in the spring, but she needed a venue to do that.

"Oh, no. What happened?"

She shrugged. "Someone else wanted that date, and they had more money than I do. It happens, unfortunately. So I'm starting over."

"I'm sorry, but if anyone can find you a new location, it's Becca."

"That's what I'm hoping." She slid her phone onto the trunk that doubled as a coffee table. "Back to you. Are you going to be okay?"

I didn't really have a choice. "I will. Eventually." Leaning back, I hugged an olive-green pillow to my chest. "This day has just really sucked."

"I know, sweetie. But as the saying goes, tomorrow is another day."

Bolting upright, I buried my face in the pillow. "And my first game," I mumbled into the material.

"What now?" Donna said.

"It's the first game," I repeated, lifting my head. "Which means I have to see Ryan."

Donna leaned her elbows on her knees. "The guy you went out with?"

Now I had to explain this again. "Yes, the guy I went out with. The one I lied to and now he's mad at me."

"Hold on. You lied?"

This was so embarrassing. "When we first met, he asked me what I do. I panicked and said I work in a bookstore."

Lips pursed, she said, "Hon, why would you do that?"

Each time I repeated this idiocy it sounded more ridiculous than the last time. "I didn't want him to assume that I was boring because I'm a librarian."

"And working in a bookstore sounds better somehow?"

"It did in the moment."

Rolling with my answer, she said, "So now you have to tell him the truth."

"Oh, he knows. He found out this morning when we

were introduced at the main branch. I was there to sit in on some interviews, while he was there as the consultant who gets to decide if my programs get cut." Still a tad bitter, I added, "He never told me he's a consultant. His sister said he's had some bad experiences when people find out so he doesn't say so up front."

"Then how can he be mad? He did the same thing you did."

"I don't think he sees it that way. His sister said once he calms down he'll probably give me a chance to explain, but I'm not counting on it."

"You know his sister?"

"She was one of the interviewees. She was going to help me talk to him, but then I saw Cassie and I couldn't let her get away again. By the time I raced downstairs, they were gone."

Donna rose off the couch. "Woman, you've earned some empty calories today." Crossing the short distance to the kitchen, she pulled two spoons out of a drawer before opening the freezer drawer on her fridge. When she returned, she shoved a cold pint of double chocolate fudge ice cream into my hand. "Dig in."

Not the healthiest dinner, but she was right. I'd earned this treat. Tossing the lid onto the trunk, I leaned back and loaded a spoonful of chocolate goodness into my mouth.

"Remember when my life really was boring?" I said as the first bite went down.

"Your life was never boring, Megan. That's just some bullshit idea you got from your idiot ex."

Loading up my spoon, I said, "Fletcher isn't an idiot. He's just insecure and a little lost."

Dark eyes went wide. "That's a very enlightened assessment. Generous, too."

I didn't bother to say Ryan had made the observation first. Ironic thinking about it now. He called Fletcher insecure while he himself wasn't confident enough to be honest about what he did. And neither was I. We were all just kids stuck in adult bodies pretending we knew who we were when none of us had a clue.

Maybe someday we would all figure it out. I would gladly fast forward to that time because this learning as I went was getting painful.

CHAPTER EIGHTEEN

I'D LOVE TO SAY I WOKE UP FRIDAY MORNING FEELING better about the day before, but I did not. After leaving Donna's, I called Dad on the way home to share how poorly the meeting with Cassie had gone. As expected, his first response was that he would contact Geraldine and straighten things out. That was the last thing I wanted.

Getting to know my long-lost siblings would be wonderful, of course, but that didn't mean I wanted my mother back in my life. She'd made her choice long ago, and the letter had reiterated what I already knew. I was a mistake from her past, and that's where she intended for me to stay. I'd done what I needed to do. I told Cassie the truth. What that would trigger I had no idea, but I would keep Dad out of the fray as much as I could.

The day ahead may not have held the same trials, but

the knots in my stomach would remain until I got through the next encounter with Ryan. If Rachel was right, his initial anger had likely faded, but there was no guarantee. I understood why he left out a few details, and if he couldn't understand why I'd done the same—or changed the details, to be fair—then I'd accept that.

I wouldn't be happy, but I would survive, which felt like progress. At least in my head.

"Good morning," said Miriam with her boundless cheer. "How are we doing today?"

I tried to meet her level of positivity with little success. "I'm okay. How are you?"

"You don't sound okay and we'll get to that, but first…" She held out her wrist, which was adorned with shiny new hardware.

"Let me see." I pulled her arms closer. "It's gorgeous. Devon, I assume?"

A giggle escaped her pale-pink lips. "Of course. He's too good to me, but I'm not complaining." Sobering, she crossed her arms. "Now, what is going on with you? I've been so busy that I feel like it's been weeks since we checked in. What ever happened with that new man of yours?"

This conversation was going to take a while. "Not great, but it's mostly my own fault. Do you ever get weird reactions when you tell men that you're a librarian?"

Dark eyes rolled so hard her lash extensions touched her eyebrows. "Good heavens. I've gotten everything from 'You must be a tiger in bed' to 'Do you do naked story time?'"

Again, not exactly my experience. "What about the other direction? Assuming you must be a boring prude?"

With pursed lips, she tilted her head. "No, I haven't heard that one."

So maybe I just *looked* boring and the job had nothing to do with it. That would have been a helpful revelation a few weeks ago.

"Anyway, to delay that kind of reaction, I didn't tell Ryan up front that I'm a librarian. And *before* I could tell him, he found out by accident yesterday, when I also found out he wasn't completely truthful either."

Miriam dropped into her chair. "I feel like I should have a bucket of popcorn for whatever comes next."

I'd prefer this to be a movie script and not my very real life.

"Guess who the consultant is?"

"The consultant?"

"The one deciding on the fate of our programs."

She popped back to her feet. "No way."

"Yes way. We ran into each other at the main branch when I was on my way upstairs for the interviews. I'm sure you can imagine how that went."

"I'm scared to even ask."

The memory still made me cringe. "I was angry. He was angry. Jeffrey was confused and asked if we knew each other. That's when Ryan said something to the tune of 'I thought we did, but I was wrong.' He then walked off, and I stood there feeling like the idiot that I am." Lifting my teacup in salute, I added, "In other words, it did not go well."

Lowering slowly back into her chair, Miriam said, "I'm so sorry. He sounded like a nice guy after that disastrous date you had."

"He's still a nice guy. He just isn't going to be *my* nice guy. Our first game is tonight and I have no idea what to say to him, but I'm not going to grovel. I screwed up, but he wasn't totally honest either."

"Incoming," said Thomas as he approached the counter. "Jeffrey asked me to bring this up."

"What is it?" Miriam asked.

Thomas shrugged. "I don't know. He just said give this to Ms. Knox."

Was the insufferable man ever going to learn my first name? I took the manila folder and untied the string that held it shut. One sheet of paper slid out upside down and I flipped it.

Mitchell and Minkowicz Consulting Group was scrawled across the top and the subject line made my lungs tighten.

"What?" Miriam said. "What does it say?"

I grew angrier with every word I read. This was the outcome report from the meeting the day before, and at the top of the list of suggested cuts was the children's reading program.

"That son of a bitch," I snapped, slamming the paper down on the counter.

Both Thomas and Miriam made shushing noises. "You can't say that in here," he reminded me.

Ignoring the warning, I bolted from my chair. "There has to be a way to appeal this."

"Appeal what?" Miriam snagged the paper and read for herself. "Holy shit."

"What is with you two?" Thomas said, leaning farther over the counter.

"They're going to cut the reading program," she answered, holding the paper out for him to read as well. "I can't believe they'd do this. That program has been running for one hundred and twenty-five years. And it doesn't even cost us enough to make it worth cutting. What is the point?"

"These are just suggested cuts," Thomas pointed out. "That doesn't mean they'll happen for sure."

"Oh, they'll happen. Jeffrey doesn't care two bits for these programs. He'll do whatever they tell him, and screw the patrons who will lose out."

"What about that report you did? Didn't you list everything in order of importance?" Miriam waved the report in the air. "It's like they totally ignored you."

"Guys, I think it's a little early to panic," Thomas said. "We don't know how seriously the higher-ups will take these suggestions."

I appreciated Thomas' optimism, but this was exactly the time to panic. Or rather, to form a plan.

Dropping into my seat, I slid up to my keyboard. "We're going to fight this."

"How?" the pair said in unison.

"We've all been here longer than Jeffrey has. We know who to talk to to go over his head."

"Whoa," Thomas said. "Again, we don't know if any of this will be enacted. Don't you think we should talk to Jeffrey first? What if you fire off an email and find out the programs aren't being cut at all?"

He had a point. As much as I hated to do so, we needed to start with Jeffrey on the slim chance that he'd pushed back against the recommendations.

"Fine. Let's go see what he says." When Miriam and I reached the top of the stairs, I realized Thomas wasn't with us. Turning around, I found him lingering at the desk. "Aren't you coming?"

He gave a sheepish look. "Someone has to stay here."

"Coward," Miriam muttered.

"We can do this," I said, tugging her along.

At the base of the stairs, we made the left and I knocked on our boss' door. No answer came. I knocked again and still, only silence.

"Did he leave?" Miriam whispered.

"It's barely ten o'clock. He didn't mention any meetings, and it's too early for lunch."

I knocked one more time, harder than before, and Ms. Patty popped up behind us.

"He's gone," she said, startling both me and Miriam. "Sorry, ladies. I didn't mean to scare you."

"Did you say Jeffrey is gone?" I asked.

"I saw him leave a few minutes after Thomas came out of his office." She pointed to the meeting room across the hall. "I watched him through the doorway. He had his trench coat and briefcase in hand so I assume he left for the day."

Miriam and I stared at each other.

"He knew we'd come down, didn't he?"

A muscle twitched in my jaw as I nodded. "I'm sure of it. If he planned to save the programs, he wouldn't have had any reason to avoid us."

"Save the programs?" Patty repeated.

This was not set in stone, and the last thing we needed was to start an uproar from the parents who counted on us.

"It's nothing," I said. "Just some internal library stuff." Shoving Miriam into motion, I pushed her back to the stairs. "The kids should start coming in any minute. I'll be back down as soon as I take care of one thing upstairs."

Patty didn't respond as we hurried away.

"What are we going to do?" Miriam mumbled loud enough for only me to hear.

"Exactly what I said before. Going over his head."

"Jeffrey isn't going to like that."

"Good," I snapped. "Maybe he'll quit in protest."

———

OF ALL THE days for me not to be able to play in a game, this was the worst, because by the time I reached the field, I was running on raw fury. Did I blame Jeffrey alone for cutting the reading program? Absolutely not. I didn't spend all that time on a report showing exactly where funds could be saved and where cutting would be a mistake to be completely ignored.

I expected as much from Jeffrey. He didn't care about our patrons, especially the kids. At this point, I wasn't even sure why he took the job. His previous experience was in corporate America, and managing libraries was more about people than the bottom line. The man was the wrong person for the position, but I could fight only one battle at a time and I'd get to that one once the program was saved.

The recommendation I read this morning came straight from Ryan. He'd read a summary that described how much that program benefited underserved children and still recommended letting it go. Who does that?

Because I was still a member of the team, I wore my uniform—the black T-shirt coach handed out at the start of the last practice plus black sweatpants—and planned to sit on the bench, safe in the assumption that Ryan wouldn't give me the time of day. I would wait until *after* the game to tell him exactly what I thought of him and his version of *consulting*.

What I did not expect was for my friends to show up with their bag chairs and tumblers in hand. The drinks looked like soda, but I knew better than to assume at least a few weren't spiked with something stronger than carbonation.

"Why are you guys here?" I asked as the rest of my team warmed up on the field.

Josie dropped into her navy-blue chair and slid her drink into the cupholder. "Donna filled us in, and we all agreed that you needed our support."

"I'm not even playing."

"Not that kind of support," Lindsey said, fighting to get her chair to sit level. "Where is this hypocritical man?"

"Guys—"

"Is that Fletcher's girlfriend?" Becca said with awe in her voice.

I turned to see Fiona drop a kiss on Fletcher's lips before strolling into center field with a smile on her face. Looked like they might work out after all.

"That's her. Gorgeous, isn't she?"

Donna used her hand to shield against the setting sun. "Who? Which one is she?"

"Center field," Josie said.

A second later, Donna whistled. "I need to get that woman on film."

"I told you." Returning to the reason they were here, I said, "I don't need support to deal with Ryan. If anything, he's going to need protection from me."

"What did he do now?" Becca asked.

Not wanting to be overheard, I bent down and signaled for them to lean in. "I got the consultant report this morning. He recommended that we cut the children's program."

"That bastard," Lindsey said loud enough for spectators ten feet away to hear.

"Keep it down. I have no plans to make a scene before the game is over."

"Does that mean there will be a scene *after* the game?" Donna asked.

I straightened and crossed my arms. "That depends on Ryan. I intend to let him know where he can stick his recommendation. How he responds will determine what comes next."

Josie made a purring sound. "Claws out and ready to fight. I'm so glad we came."

The team gathered in the dugout, signaling the game was about to start.

"I need to get in there. It's sweet that you're here, but you don't have to stay."

"Are you kidding?" Donna said, pulling a bag of corn

chips from her purse. "We're here for the duration, woman."

"Do you have salsa for those?" Lindsey asked.

Pulling a glass container from her bag, Donna said, "Of course I do."

"Should I even ask what's in those cups?" I said.

"Mine is just pop," Josie said, "I'm the designated driver. I can't account for the rest of these lushes."

Donna waved the words away. "A dash of Jack does not make us lushes. The extra bottle in the car for refills might."

"Just don't do anything to embarrass me."

Lindsey loaded salsa onto a chip. "We make no promises."

Returning to the dugout, I couldn't help but laugh. No matter how crappy my life was, I always had the girls to make me smile. Man, I loved them. *They* were my family, and I wouldn't trade them for all the mothers in the world.

———

THE BRAVADO I'd shown with the girls waned a bit once I was in the same space with Ryan. As I'd assumed, he pretended I wasn't there. Fine by me. Or so I told myself. In truth, the slight hurt more than I liked, but this was no longer about my personal life. This was about my job and the kids I had to fight for.

Also as expected, we beat the other team with no problem. A little disappointing considering I had nothing to do with it. Not that I wanted us to lose, or that I thought I was such a crucial player that they couldn't win without me. I just wished my replacement hadn't been quite so good. Brenda Marsh had been pulled in from the outfield and played well enough for me to wonder if I'd have to compete for the position once I came back.

Tempted to tell Coach I was good to go right away, I flexed my ankle and pain shot up my shin. The temptation went away.

By the seventh inning, we were up by ten runs and the game ended there. Handshakes were exchanged, gear packed up, and my stomach churned with nerves. Was I really going to do this? I pictured Ruby's face, beautiful and imperfect and full of wonder, and I had my answer. The timing had to be just right. Preferably *off* the field and away from the others. That meant following him to the parking lot and making my stand there.

A bit stalkerish, but the best plan I could come up with.

Coach made the announcement that the team had done well enough for us to skip the Monday practice, but to gather next Wednesday to work out a few kinks and review what we knew about our next opponent. Everyone headed for the parking lot, and I walked out of the dugout to find my friends waiting. Chairs on their shoulders and cups in hand, they were ready to have my back. Ryan walked ahead of me, so I pointed him out as subtly as I could and they got the message. I kept going since I couldn't let him get too far ahead.

When he reached his car and popped the trunk, I knew it was now or never.

CHAPTER NINETEEN

"I NEED TO TALK TO YOU," I SAID, STEPPING UP TO the car.

"There isn't anything to talk about," he said, dropping his gear bag in and closing the trunk.

Oh, but there was. "This isn't about us. This is about the library."

Ryan crossed his arms and leaned a hip on the car. "What about it?"

"How could you cut a program that is so important?"

Still playing Mr. Nonchalant, he said, "I didn't cut anything. I made recommendations, which is my job to do. What they choose to cut or keep is up to them."

He would not get off that easy. "You knew when you made that list what would happen. Don't try to absolve yourself of the responsibility now. Those kids need our program."

"What kids?"

Red-hot fury raced through my veins. Did he really care so little about what I did that he didn't even remember his own report?

"The kids who rely on my library's reading program. The ones who need a safe space after school. The ones who need educational resources they can't get anywhere else. The ones you clearly don't give a crap about, you heartless jerk."

Ryan straightened and held up his hands. "Hold on. The information I was given said participation in that program had dropped to the point that only one or two children came in per week. The summary also said personnel were often being paid to sit in an empty room when the kids didn't show at all. That's what my decision was based on. Are you saying that isn't the case?"

None of that was true. "We have a full room several days a week. Many of them come from struggling families and attend underfunded schools. Plus, other than our staff, who would be on the clock either way, adults who come specifically to help the program are volunteers. They aren't costing the library a penny." So that he couldn't get away with his bogus claim, I added, "*All of which* I put in my report, so I know you had the facts."

"I don't know anything about your report, but the documentation Jeffrey Chamberlain provided looked nothing like what you just described."

"What are you talking about? My report should have been what Jeffrey gave you."

"Megan, I'm telling you. That is not what I read."

He'd had my summary in plenty of time for the meeting. An entire two days before, in fact. Mind racing, I struggled to make sense of what Ryan was saying. Then the realization dawned. Two days was plenty of time for Jeffrey to edit the report to say whatever he wanted. There would be enough facts to sound accurate, but with enough lies to throw the programs he didn't want under the proverbial consultant bus.

"That son of a…" To Ryan, I said, "Can I get a copy of what you received?"

"I'm not sure that's—"

"Ryan, it's all lies. I can almost guarantee it. But the only way I can prove that is to get a copy of what you saw." Hoping he wasn't the heartless jerk I'd made him out to be, I said, "I have to fight for my kids. Please, help me do that."

After a brief hesitation, he nodded. "Text me your email and I'll send it."

Forming a plan in my mind, I said, "Thank you."

As I walked away, he said, "Megan. I'm sorry."

I turned back. "You didn't know he was lying."

He shook his head. "Not just about that. About all of it."

The least I could do was offer the same. "Me, too. I'm sorry I wasn't honest from the beginning." Sensing a possibility for this to turn around, I remembered some-thing he'd once said. "Would it be crazy to ask if we can start over?" Extending a hand, I said, "Hi, I'm Megan Knox and I'm a librarian."

Lips curving in that slow smile that made my heart stutter, he took my hand. "I'm Ryan Stallings. I'm a consultant and can be an idiot sometimes."

His warm hand enveloped mine as I offered another truth. "Then we have something in common." Growing serious, I added, "I really like you, and I really am sorry that I didn't have the confidence to be myself from the start. If you give me another shot, I promise to do better."

"Same here." Looking down at his dirty uniform, he said, "If you don't mind a little sweat, I know a good ice cream shop not far from here. What do you say?"

I didn't mind at all. "I'd love some ice cream."

"Then I'll text you the name. Meet me there?"

More optimistic than I'd felt in days, I nodded. "I can do that."

I backed away toward my car and as I spun with a smile on my face, the girls broke out in applause. I'd totally forgotten they were there. Embarrassed but too happy to be mad at them, I brought them quickly up to date, and then raced off with a small part of my brain still on the Jeffrey issue. Once I had the evidence in hand, I knew exactly what I would do with it. With any luck, Mr. Chamberlain would not be my problem for much longer.

WHEN I'D FOLLOWED Ryan to the parking lot, I hadn't expected to fix anything between us. I hadn't even been sure that was possible. Finding out he wasn't a heartless schmuck who would take books away from children did help. We'd both been idiots so it wasn't as if I could hold a grudge. Especially not after his apology.

But that didn't mean we had nothing else to work out. So far, our brief relationship had been anything but smooth, and since two restarts were more than enough, it was time to get everything out in the open.

"I'll be thirty in a few weeks, I'm a Libra, and I dislike both cilantro and mint chocolate anything," I said, wrapping up my speech, which might have included a few too many details. "Oh, and I hate pickles. Can't even stand the smell of them."

Ryan's rich laughter matched the ice cream in his cup —a chocolate concoction called Pittsburgh Pot Holes. "I'm a Taurus, I'll be thirty-three next April, and I forgive you for not liking pickles. I could eat them every day."

I knew he was too good to be true.

"That's it. This will never work out."

He sat up straighter. "I don't have to eat them every day. How about if I only have them when you aren't around or at least keep them away from your nose?"

His willingness to sacrifice won me over. "I accept that compromise." We were dancing around the real topic. "Not that I have any excuse for lying about the librarian thing, but I would like to explain."

"Rachel told me some of it. Do people really make those kinds of assumptions?"

"They do, but I'm sure there are assumptions made about all sorts of jobs. My problem was that I liked you, and I wanted to keep you interested long enough to get to know me before learning what I do."

Setting his cup on the metal table between us, Ryan stabbed the pink plastic spoon into his ice cream. "I liked you, too. From the minute you slammed that bat into my chest, I thought this is a girl I'd like to know."

"No, you didn't."

"Yes, I did. The minute you turned around, all big brown eyes and that cute little nose, I was a goner."

For once, I didn't mind the word *cute*.

"Now that I'm blushing, it's your turn. Rachel told me a bit about why you don't use the consultant title right away either. I admit, I might have been a little less interested, but only because that was the same day I found out the library system had hired a consultant to review the programs." Quite the coincidence looking back now. "I had no idea it was you, of course."

"Knowing what we know now, that part was for the best. We couldn't have gone out while the review was going on." He lifted his ice cream once more. "I'm still not proud of misleading you."

Digging a chunk of pound cake out of my dessert, I

said, "From now on then, total honesty. Which means I need to tell you one more thing."

He gave me his full attention. "What is it?"

"Fletcher told me he wants me back."

His deep-brown eyes held mine. "What did you say?"

"I told him he needed to spend some time on himself and that we were never right for each other."

Ryan visibly relaxed, which gave my ego a much-needed boost. "That's good to know." After a brief silence, he asked, "Why did you stay with him for so long?"

Oddly enough, I had an answer for this. "I know it sounds strange, but I think it goes back to my mother. She was a huge personality. Maybe not as big as in my memories, since to a child everything is exaggerated, but Geraldine was bubbly and bold and loved attention. I'm pretty sure that I thought that being with Fletcher would make me more like her. Like, his personality would rub off on me or something."

Appearing to absorb my answer, Ryan nodded. "I can see that. But I like you just the way you are. Smart, fierce, kind. Those are much better qualities to have."

If he was trying to make me cry in my ice cream, he was doing a bang-up job. "I'm really glad you moved here."

Sexy grin firmly in place, he leaned forward on the table. "Me, too."

———

NOT LONG AFTER I got home the night before, still floating from the ice cream excursion, Jeffrey's version of the programming report landed in my inbox. Just as I'd suspected, he'd kept enough details for the information to appear legit, while changing or deleting crucial data on three different programs. All ones that used the meeting room across from his office.

Was the man seriously sabotaging much-needed programming because of proximity to his office? Really?

I spent Saturday morning comparing the two reports —mine and his edited version—to note every discrepancy and omission. I'd also made sure to highlight all of the direct falsehoods he'd included. Whatever his motives, this wasn't only unfair to our patrons, but unethical, and I was sure a breach with the consulting firm to supply accurate and truthful documentation.

Once my findings were emailed to both the library system director and the head of Human Resources, I started my laundry and settled in with a book to kill the hours before Ryan would pick me up. We were doing dinner and a movie, and it felt good to know there were no more secrets between us.

When my doorbell rang unexpectedly, I checked the clock, fearful that I'd lost track of time. I hadn't. There was more than an hour to go before he would pick me up. Hurrying down the stairs, I looked through the peephole to see the back of a woman's head. Probably someone taking a survey or wanting to tell me about their candidate. I headed back upstairs, but the bell rang again, and something told me I needed to answer it or they would keep pushing that dang button.

Caving, I dragged the door open, but I could not have been remotely prepared for the person I found on the other side. Though I hadn't even looked at a picture of her in years, I recognized the eyes, the nose, the haughty way she held her head.

This was my mother.

Stunned into silence, I stared, unable to believe my eyes. Was she a figment of my imagination? If I closed the door and opened it again, would she be gone?

"Are you going to invite me in?" she said in greeting. The edge in her voice made the hair on my arms stand up. She was definitely real.

Her silver-tinged dark hair was pulled back into a tight bun, accentuating her blue eyes, which I realized matched Cassie's exactly. The tapered jeans were a dark denim, and the plum jacket tossed over a simple peach top created a business casual look.

The glare, however, was anything but casual.

"What are you doing here?"

"I'm not discussing this through a doorway."

Part of my brain reverted to seven-year-old me, intimidated and anxious to please her. The other part said hell no did she get to show up at my door and make demands now.

"What exactly are we discussing?" I asked, standing my ground.

Clearly annoyed, she attempted to stare through me. I stared back. Caving first, she said, "I'm here to discuss what you told Cassie."

"I told Cassie the truth."

"Did you consider what hearing that would do to her?"

"Did you consider what leaving would do to me?"

Jaw tight, she flinched but ignored my question. "I have a flight out in two hours. Are you going to let me in or not?"

The temptation to slam the door was overwhelming. At the same time, this would likely be my only chance to have this conversation, and though she might not answer my questions, I still deserved the opportunity to ask them.

Stepping back, I said, "Follow me."

Halfway up the stairs, I heard the door click shut, followed by the beat of her footsteps behind me. Memories flashed through my mind. Of sundresses and panty-hose. Heady perfume and fancy heels lined up along the back wall of a tiny closet. Hats and scarves and big round sunglasses that had made me feel like I was riding around with a movie star.

She'd been everything I wanted to be back then. Today, I wanted to be nothing like her.

I'd straightened the house in anticipation of Ryan's arrival, though I didn't care in that moment what she thought of my home. She hadn't been very domestic in those early years, nor had she stuck around to teach me the finer elements of interior design.

"You're in," I said, not bothering to offer her a drink or to invite her to sit down. "What did you want to say?"

"You had no business talking to Cassie like that."

"She's my sister," I reminded her. "She deserved to know that."

Lips tight, the white-knuckle grip on her purse strap revealed how tightly she was gripping her temper. A memory flashed again. Like a scene from a movie, I saw her screaming like a madwoman and throwing all the pretty shoes from the closet over my head. Eyes dropping to the floor, I shook the visions away.

"What did you think was going to happen?" Geraldine said, drawing closer like a cat approaching its prey. "That she would believe *you* over *me*? She doesn't know you, Megan. You're a stranger to her."

"Thanks to you." She'd robbed us all of so much. "What I told her was the truth. Your leaving didn't change who I am."

"Oh, please. You were the result of a mindless decision driven by teenage lust and too much alcohol. I never even liked James. My parents forced me to marry him because of *you*. And then *you* turned out to be just like him. Dull. Meek. Ordinary. Always with your nose in a book or your head in the clouds. You never felt like my daughter. You felt like what you were. A mistake."

Every word cut like a razor blade across my skin. If she hated me that much, I couldn't help but wonder why she'd stayed as long as she had.

"You never loved me at all." This wasn't a revelation, but the first time I'd said the words aloud. "I was an innocent child. You chose to crawl into the back seat of that car. What happened after was the result of *your* decision. You can't blame me for any of it."

She shook her head, not hearing me at all. "Everything changed because of you. I had dreams. Ambitions. Do you think I wanted to stay in that dinky little town?"

Pointing out the obvious, I said, "We could have all moved together."

"That never would have worked. I'd still have been trapped in that marriage. And I couldn't have done any of the things I wanted to do with you along. I had to get out."

So much became clear in my mind. She'd spun a narrative that worked for her. One that was only true in the world she'd created in her mind. A world where I didn't fit, so she'd written me out as if I never existed. Seeing who she was now, I was almost grateful. Geraldine had done me a favor by walking away.

"I don't know what you told Cassie," I said, "but someday she'll figure it out and she'll realize who you really are. As for me, I might be a regret to you, but I was *never* a mistake." Walking past her to reach the door, I held it open. "This conversation is over. You need to leave."

"Not until you promise never to contact Cassie ever again."

As if she had any power to force that promise. "I said you need to leave. Now."

"I said—"

"Now!" I snapped. *"Get out of my house."*

Blue eyes went wide before she stormed past me. "Contact her and you'll be dealing with me," she warned on her way down the stairs.

Instead of responding with a phrase I never used, I slammed the door loud enough to earn a pounding on the ceiling downstairs. Augie would have to get over it. Seconds passed as I stared at my floor while adrenaline ebbed from my bloodstream.

Geraldine's brutal words had numbed me. Maybe it was the shock of hearing how she really felt. The contempt in her voice, as if I was a curse that had tried to ruin her life. But as the numbness wore off, pain flowed in to take its place. Years of believing that I was the reason she left only to learn that I was. Just not in any rational, sane way.

Before I realized what was happening, I was on the floor with tears running off my chin. All of the questions. All of the years spent yearning for a mother who loved me. Who wanted me. They all crashed around me until I curled into a ball, my forehead pressed against my knees as I wailed like a wounded, helpless creature. My breath hitched and I couldn't stop. I couldn't stop the hurt consuming me.

Sobs turned to whimpers, whimpers turned to hiccups, and I was finally able to sit back up. Crawling to the coffee table, I grabbed the box of tissues to wipe my face and blow my nose. Lashes still wet, I leaned back against the couch and dropped my head onto the cushion. My sinuses weren't happy, but as I took several deep breaths, I felt lighter.

Still hurt, but not the crushing pain of before, I couldn't believe she was really here. That she'd been standing right in front of me after twenty-three years. I pinched myself to make sure I hadn't been dreaming. Or rather, in the middle of a nightmare. Playing the whole thing back, I had an odd feeling. I was proud of myself. There had been a time when I'd have handled that encounter very differently. I couldn't control what Geraldine would tell Cassie, or if Cassie would ever contact me again, but I didn't regret telling her.

Even after that horrible experience. I did the right thing. That's all that mattered.

CHAPTER TWENTY

MY EYES WERE STILL RED AND SWOLLEN WHEN RYAN rang my doorbell. I repaired the damage with makeup as best I could, but he knew the moment I opened the door that I'd been crying. I relayed the scene with Geraldine, leaving out the harshest parts, and by the time I wrapped up with me kicking my prodigal mother out of my house, I'd decided to change the plan for the night ahead.

"Do you mind if we skip the movie and do something else before dinner?"

"We can skip the whole thing if you don't want to go," Ryan replied. We were sitting on my couch as we had the night of our first date. "I wouldn't blame you after all that."

I was not calling off this date. "No, I'm not letting Geraldine take another minute from my life, but there is something I need to do to close that chapter for good."

Holding my hand, he said, "Tell me what it is, and we'll do it."

"We'll have to go downtown."

Ryan rolled to his feet and then pulled me up with him. "I'm game. Let's go."

Fifteen minutes later, we were strolling across the damp green grass of Point State Park, known as The Point to locals. This was a beautiful stretch of greenery situated at the very point where the Monongahela, Allegheny, and Ohio rivers met. Hence the name. To the east was the looming skyscrapers of downtown. To the west was the sunset over the Ohio River.

At the apex of the triangular park sat a large fountain that shot water one hundred and fifty feet into the air. This was my destination. As we stepped from grass to concrete, I stopped.

"I haven't been here since a few months before my seventh birthday," I said, my eyes locked on the soaring waterspout. "Geraldine brought me here that summer. She called it a girls' trip."

Ryan squeezed my hand. "That was right before she left, wasn't it?"

He'd been paying attention. "Yes. We walked all over downtown and ended up here. My feet were aching, but she kept going. I was happy when we got here that I could sit down on these stairs."

When I didn't move, Ryan said, "Are we going any closer?"

I wanted to. But I also wanted to run the other way. "That day isn't a great memory for me," I explained. "I just need a minute."

"Take your time." He lifted my hand and kissed the back of it before standing in silence, patiently waiting for me to decide the next move.

"I'm glad you're here with me," I said.

I'd considered returning to this site countless times over the years. The girls would have stood by me for support. Dad, who still had no idea what happened on that trip, would have come if I'd asked. At some point, I'd decided never to come back, but after today, I needed to replace that memory, and this felt like the right way to do that.

Meeting my gaze, he smiled. "Me, too."

Ready, I stepped forward and we descended the two sets of stairs that brought us closer to the fountain. As the wind shifted, a light spray hit my cheeks. I stopped again a few feet from the large concrete rim of the fountain.

"It was hot that day," I began. "We were well into summer and this entire area was packed with people. Kids were playing. I remember one little girl bumped into me and dropped her doll. I tried to pick it up to return it, but Geraldine pulled me away. She wanted to get to the fountain." Closing my eyes, I could hear the people chattering as if they were here with us. The laughter. A dog barking. "I wanted to sit and watch the people, but she only wanted to be near the water. When we finally got down here, she did something I hadn't expected."

Opening my eyes, I stared into the white burst of water.

"I've got you," Ryan said, squeezing my hand once more. "You're safe with me."

His words helped. I took a step closer and lifted my face as the water spray grew stronger.

"Geraldine was so excited to be here, she kicked off her shoes and climbed up to walk along this rim. She insisted that I climb up with her, but I didn't want to. I was too afraid of falling in or getting into trouble. No one else was up there like she was, and I noticed several in the crowd watching us."

My heart sped up as the memory played on, getting closer to the worst part.

"I kept asking her to get down, and she got sterner, demanding that I stop being a baby and come up. That was her favorite reprimand. I was always being a baby about something. If I didn't want to eat this food or swing that high, I was just being a baby. That day, I didn't care what she called me. I wanted her back on the ground and when I started crying, she finally did come down. And then smacked me across the face."

"Jesus," Ryan mumbled. "Megan, that is not okay."

"I know that now. I guess I felt it back then, but it wasn't the first time. Just the first time she'd done it in front of other people." Chest tight, I took a deep breath and slowly blew it out. "Dad still doesn't know. He'd never forgive himself if he did."

"Did you tell anyone?" he asked.

There had been *one*. "My kindergarten teacher, Mrs. Alvarez. She told the principal, who called our house. The next week, Mrs. Alvarez was replaced by Mrs. Peters, and I learned not to say anything again."

Turning me to face him, Ryan pulled me against his chest. "This is probably the worst thing to say right now, but I'm glad she left you."

As painful as this was, I couldn't help but laugh. "Life did get better once she was gone, but I still longed for her to come back. Kids are eternal optimists in that way." Leaning back far enough to look into his eyes, I said, "Thank you for letting me steal part of our date to do this. It was time to change what this place means for me. To exorcise some demons, I guess. I feel better already."

Brushing a thumb along my chin, he said, "There's one more thing we could do to make sure we've fully erased that memory."

The twinkle in his eyes made my heart flutter. "What do you suggest?"

Without a word, he leaned forward and I stopped breathing. When his lips touched mine, they were soft and gentle and made no demands. That didn't mean I couldn't make a few of my own. Sliding my hands up his chest, I wrapped them around his neck as I rose onto my tiptoes. I deepened the kiss as the wind shifted and pelted us with cold water. Breaking apart, we were both laughing as we hurried to put more distance between us and the fountain.

Breathless and happier than I'd been in a long, long time, I tugged him back up the stairs, ignoring the droplets falling from my hair. "We need to get back to this date. I'm starving."

"I'll feed you anything you want, but I have no complaints about this date so far."

Tucking in against his side, I leaned my head against his shoulder. "Neither do I."

I walked into work on Monday morning more optimistic than when I'd left on Friday. At the time, I'd had three major uncertainties in my life, and now I was down to two. The Cassie thing was still up in the air, but I'd done all I could. The rest was up to her. I did pay Dad a visit on Sunday to tell him about Geraldine. He was upset that I hadn't called the moment she showed up at my door, but there wouldn't have been anything he could do. She'd have been gone by the time he got there.

Plus, I wouldn't have wanted him to hear whatever toxic rationalizations she'd have thrown his way. Everything was my fault or Dad's fault or even her parents' fault. Geraldine bore no culpability at all for her own choices, and that made even trying to talk to her pointless. A lesson I learned the hard way, but at least it was over with now and I could get on with my life.

I still didn't tell him about the abuse. There was no point now.

"Good morning," said Miriam as she plopped into her chair. "Though I guess we have yet to see if it's good or not."

My email to the directors had not been answered so I had to agree. This day could go either way. The kids would always be welcome at the library, whether the program was cut or not, but many of the resources they currently enjoyed, as well as some one-on-one attention the program provided, would go away. If the final word came down, I fully intended to fight on to reverse the decision.

An hour into the day, the elevator opened and three familiar faces stepped out. Meredith Fellows, the system director; Regina Norman, the director of Human Resources; and the man who kissed me senseless two nights before, Ryan Stallings.

"Good morning," I said, leaping from my seat and hopping to attention.

Director Fellows did not look pleased. "Good morning, Megan. Is Chamberlain here?"

"He came in half an hour ago." The expressions on the two women's faces gave nothing away. A ball of nerves, I shot Ryan a questioning look. When he winked, the knot in my stomach loosened. "Do you want me to call him up here?"

The director shook her head. "That won't be necessary, but do you have time to accompany us to his office?"

As if I'd say no to witnessing whatever was about to happen. "I do, yes."

Sliding around a speechless Miriam, I quickly whispered, "I think we're going to be okay." Gesturing toward the stairs, I let the three visitors go first, but Ryan lingered behind so we were side by side. When he wiggled his brows and smiled, I nearly giggled with excitement. This was going to be good.

Once we were all downstairs, Regina Norman knocked on Jeffrey's closed door. "What is it?" he barked from the other side.

The two women exchanged a telling glance before Regina turned the doorknob and we stepped inside. There wasn't room for all of us so I remained in the doorway with a clear view of the action.

The HR director tossed a folder onto his desk as Jeffrey bolted from his chair, his eyes wide and mouth agape. "What's this about?"

"Did you falsify the programs report submitted to the consultant?" Director Fellows asked. Her tone said she knew the answer, but she gave him the chance to respond anyway. I believed this was called giving him the rope and letting him hang himself.

"I don't know what you're talking about." His eyes cut from me to Ryan and back to the director. "Everything I turned over was accurate."

Unflinching, Director Fellows said, "I've reviewed both the original report, supplied by Ms. Knox, and the one submitted to Mr. Stallings. The one that has your name at the top. There are some troubling discrepancies between the two." Before he could respond, she added, "I've also compared the one Ms. Knox created to our library data and found hers to be impressively accurate. Can you explain why yours is not?"

Like a cornered animal, he sputtered, "All of my information came from her." A chubby finger pointed in my direction. "If it's wrong, then that's what she gave me. She must have given you a corrected version to make me look bad."

The ladies weren't buying it.

Regina slipped another folder onto his desk. "You have exactly fifteen minutes to vacate this office, Mr. Chamberlain. Your employment here has been terminated."

"You can't do that," he blubbered. "On what grounds?"

Director Fellows took a step forward. "We've done a little more research into your references and employment history. Behavior like mishandling of funds and sexual harassment of a coworker—all documented and corroborated—were conveniently omitted from your resume.

Adding falsifying documentation for an ongoing financial review and your termination is more than justified. I suggest you start packing up. The clock is ticking."

I knew he'd lied about the programs, but I'd never imagined he was guilty of so much more.

"Stanford Bridges will have something to say about this," Jeffrey muttered as he grabbed his trench coat off the hook behind him.

"Stanford is no longer on the Board of Trustees."

"Since when?"

"Since today," Director Fellows replied. "He won't be able to help you now. Regina will stay here to escort you out." She shifted her attention to me. "Megan, do you have time to talk?"

"Yes, ma'am. I'm free until the senior computer class starts in thirty minutes."

Another program Jeffrey had tried to cut.

"Good. Then let's take this upstairs."

———

THERE WERE no offices on the second floor, and enough patrons entering to make a private chat at the front desk impossible, so I suggested we chat in a quiet corner in the non-fiction section. I had no idea what the director wanted to talk about, other than what they planned to do now about Jeffrey's open position. Part of me hoped she might tell me that Nancy was coming back.

"First," she began, "I want to apologize for ever installing Jeffrey Chamberlain into that position. Apparently, he and Stanford Bridges are old college buddies. Fraternity brothers. This is the second time Stanford has helped him cover past indiscretions to find a job. We trusted Mr. Bridges' judgment and didn't scrutinize Chamberlain as much as we should have."

Regina Norman joined us at that moment. "He's gone," she said. "And I take responsibility for that. I made assumptions based on Stanford referring him when I shouldn't have."

"We've all learned a lesson from this," Director Fellows said. "To the point that we plan to be more thoughtful about finding his replacement. Which leads to you." She paused and I glanced over to Ryan, who had been silent through this entire scene. He offered a reassuring smile, but I had no idea what I was being reassured about. "Megan," the director went on, "we would like you to consider taking the job."

Watching Jeffrey get fired had been shocking. This left me stunned.

"Me?" I squeaked.

"Yes, you," Regina replied. "Your report on the programs showed us more than Chamberlain's deception. It shone a light on your knowledge of how the library operates, as well as the passion and devotion you have for the patrons we serve. That makes you an obvious candidate for branch manager, and we hope you agree."

This possibility never even occurred to me. Even when Nancy left, I hadn't considered applying. I liked my job. I liked interacting with the patrons, old and young, but especially the children. If I took the position, much of that would go away. It wasn't a lack of ambition on my part. I simply didn't see myself taking on such a role. At least not right now.

Treading carefully, I said, "Can I make another suggestion?"

The two women exchanged a concerned glance, but the director said, "Of course."

"I think my coworker, Miriam Webster, would be more suited to the position. She's been here longer than I have. She knows the ins and outs of this place as well as if not better than I do. And she cares deeply about those around her, both patrons and coworkers." Not wanting to offend, I added, "I do appreciate the offer, but I truly believe Miriam is a better choice."

Silence fell over our little group as my superiors considered my suggestion. If they disagreed, I had no idea what I would do. There was always the chance that they would again look outside the system for a replacement and we could end up right back where we'd been with Jeffrey. Maybe not as underhanded, but not a member of the team, so to speak.

"She does have an excellent record," Regina finally said. "What she's done with the local history project is quite impressive."

"That's Miriam's project?" Director Fellows asked.

"It is." Feeling more confident, I said, "She would be an amazing manager if given the chance."

Seemingly coming to a conclusion, the director nodded. "We'll need to have a meeting before deciding for sure, but I like this idea. Megan, thank you for bringing this Chamberlain issue to our attention and for your suggestion about Miriam." Turning to Ryan, she said, "Mr. Stallings, we appreciate you accompanying us today. Without your presence, no doubt he would have denied his part in this so you see why we found it necessary that you be here."

"I do," he said. "Happy to help clear things up. I have, of course, revised my recommendations accordingly based on the correct report supplied by Ms. Knox. That should conclude the review once again. I've enjoyed working with your staff." With a half grin, he added, "Most of the staff, anyway."

"Yes," she echoed. "Hopefully, we've rooted out the one bad apple. So we're done here. Megan, thank you again. You have a bright future here. I won't be surprised if you have my job someday."

That was a huge compliment. "Someday would be nice, but I'm very happy where I am right now."

"We like to hear that." The two women turned for the elevator and Ryan stayed behind. "Are you coming, Mr. Stallings?"

Pasting an innocent look on his face, he said, "I just

have a couple of questions for Ms. Knox. A little research I'm doing for another review."

Neither woman commented and they both stepped onto the elevator when the door opened.

"Research?" I said once they were out of sight. "How can I help you, Mr. Stallings?"

"First, you can agree to have dinner with me tomorrow."

"A date on a Tuesday night? That seems unusual."

He leaned closer and the scent of sandalwood surrounded me. "I don't want to wait until the weekend to see you again."

"You'll see me on Wednesday," I pointed out. "At practice." Flexing my ankle, I added, "I can play again."

"That isn't the same thing."

No, it wasn't. "Then I guess I can make time tomorrow, but only on one condition."

Tucking a lock behind my ear, he said, "Anything."

"That we go for ice cream again."

"Ice cream?"

"Yes."

Looking around to make sure no one was looking, he dropped a quick kiss on my lips. "We can do that."

EPILOGUE

Miriam had been acting strange all day, and though I didn't know the exact reason why, I had my suspicions.

Because today was my thirtieth birthday.

My new boss—which was so awesome to say—loved birthdays. She lived for them. I'd arrived that morning to streamers hanging from the light fixtures, trays of cookies and cupcakes covering the front desk, plus she'd put the entire staff in matching shirts meant to look like softball uniforms. They were pink and black with the words West End Readers scrawled across the front. I was given one as well, except mine had *Birthday Girl* printed across the back.

Presents had been opened—all books, of course—and by mid-afternoon we'd mostly returned to business as usual. But Miriam clearly had something up her sleeve because she had that sneaky look on her face and every time the elevator opened, she nearly leaped out of her skin. That was the other thing. She'd made one excuse after another not to return to her office downstairs.

I was choosing the children's reading picks for the rest of the month when her *surprise* finally arrived, and my heart nearly stopped at the sight. Two young people, one familiar and one not, stepped off the elevator. I was too stunned to greet them so we'd stared at each other in silence.

"Wow, Cassie, how crazy seeing you here," Miriam said, as if she hadn't known they were coming. The woman had terrible acting skills. "Who's your friend?"

Eyes on me, Cassie said, "This is my brother, Luke." To me, she said, "*Our* brother, I guess."

Tears sprang to my eyes, and the pair quickly went out of focus.

"Let's go downstairs," Miriam said, pulling me out of my chair and away from the front desk. "Cassie, you, too."

By the time we reached the break room, I'd regained some control.

"What are you doing here?" I said as Miriam slid out the door, leaving us alone.

Cassie glanced up at her brother, who looked just like her except several inches taller. Same blue eyes. Same dark-blond hair. "Well, um…" She cleared her throat and looked back my way. "I'm not sure if you remember when I mentioned that I'd found one relative through my DNA results, but he turned out to be a great uncle, and though he's really old and has dementia, his daughter responded to my message. She's my… I mean *our* mom's cousin."

Still in shock to have them standing before me, I could do little more than nod.

"She confirmed everything you said. About Mom having you when she was a teenager, to her leaving you seven years later." Rubbing her brow, she added, "I'm sorry I didn't believe you."

"No," I said, barely holding back the tears. "That was a lot to take in. I get it. I'm just…" I looked at my brother, who had yet to say a word. "I'm so happy you're here. I don't know what else to say."

"We'd like to get to know you," Luke finally said. "If that's okay with you."

Okay? This was the best birthday present I would ever receive in my whole life.

"I would really, really like that." Worried about the one person we all had in common, I asked, "Does Geraldine know you're here?"

Cassie nodded. "She does. She isn't happy, but she did admit the truth once I told her about talking to her cousin. I asked her to come with us, but she… didn't want to."

Hearing that statement didn't hurt nearly as much as it would have a few weeks ago.

Happy beyond measure, I couldn't stop staring at them. These were my siblings. My sister and brother. No longer thinking of myself as an only child was going to take some getting used to, but I looked forward to the day that this would feel normal.

"I'm not sure where to start," I said to break the awkward silence. "I have so many questions, and I'm sure you do, too, but I have a couple more hours of work left."

"No, you don't," said Miriam, storming back into the room. She shoved my coat and purse into my arms. "You're off for the rest of the day."

"But I—"

"I'm your boss and I say go home." Eyes bright and pink lips curved into a smile, she said, "Go on. You all have some catching up to do." In a whisper, she added, "Happy birthday, Megan."

Now I was going to cry again. Wrapping my arms around her, I whispered back, "Thank you so much."

Pulling away, she dabbed at her cheeks. "You're making my mascara run."

We laughed and poor Luke shifted from one foot to the other, clearly uncomfortable with all the crying. I didn't blame him.

"My apartment is a few blocks away, but I walked to work today. Do you have a car?"

"We do," Cassie said. "But we don't want to put you out. If you'd rather meet someplace later…"

I couldn't meet tonight because we were all having dinner at Dad's house. The girls, including Becca's Jacob, and Nessa with her daughter's family. I'd met them a couple weeks before and Maddox was every bit as adorable as his grandmother described him. But I didn't want to let Cassie and Luke out of my sight.

Then I realized they had to come to dinner.

———

THEY'D TAKEN SOME CONVINCING, but Cassie and Luke agreed to join my birthday celebration. Since it felt wrong to toss them into the full group on our first day of getting to know each other, the three of us had come to Dad's house an hour early so he could meet them. They actually had quite a few questions for him, since he knew more about Geraldine than any of us. At least the girl she'd been all those years ago.

"She's never told us any of these stories," Cassie said as Dad wrapped up a tale about the time Geraldine had a yelling match with one of their teachers over a research paper. I gave him credit for only sharing stories that put her in a positive light. He certainly had plenty of reasons to do the opposite.

"Your mother was popular. Not a great student, but she never lacked friends. I couldn't believe it when she agreed to go out with me." Casting a quick glance my way, he added, "That night changed both of our lives."

Not ready to go there, I said, "Tell them about her parents. I don't even know much about them."

Dad jumped into a number of stories about the Pendletons. My grandfather had managed a local grocery store and had been a church deacon. Geraldine's mother had been a schoolteacher. Both of those facts I knew, but I never knew they lost a son.

"David was older than Geri," Dad explained, "and joined the military right after high school. He was killed in the first gulf war."

"How did I never know that?" I asked.

He shook his head. "Your grandmother never got over the loss, so they didn't talk about him to keep from upsetting her. David's fiancé was the maid of honor at our wedding, but they never married because he was killed a few months later."

"I'd really like to know more about him," Luke said.

My brother had warmed up quite a bit once the three of us reached my apartment and started talking. To my delight, he relaxed even more when we reached Dad's house. The twins told me about men coming in and out of their lives, but none ever staying for long. Other than the one who'd actually adopted them, but once he and Geraldine had divorced, she'd cut him off from the kids.

Though there was no blood tie between them, I hoped

Luke and Dad might bond enough to offer him a hint of the father figure he might be longing for.

"I'm sure Jacqueline can tell us more," I said, referring to the relative who'd confirmed my story. "Her mother was our grandfather's sister, so she's bound to have photos or something."

"We hope so," Cassie said. "We're meeting up with her in a few days. I'm sure she wouldn't mind if you came."

Just then, a knock sounded at the front door, and I checked the clock. We'd been so engrossed in our conversation, I hadn't realized it was so late. Dad welcomed the other dinner guests, who all knew that Cassie and Luke were there. I'd sent a text to make sure no one was surprised.

Lindsey arrived late, as always, which was ironic considering she was the fastest driver. But then, she had to drive fast because she was always late.

The weather was warm for mid-October so we moved the gathering out to the patio. Dad had filled the space with extra chairs once Nessa and her family started coming by more often. There was only one person missing, so when another knock came, I jumped from my chair.

"I'll get it!" Ignoring the girls' laughter behind me, I hurried through the house and swept the front door open. Before me was a giant bouquet of flowers. "How pretty."

The bouquet shifted to the left as Ryan peeked around them. "Happy birthday."

Heart fluttering as it always did when I saw him, I said, "Thank you." Taking the flowers, I pulled him inside. "We're sitting out on the patio. I think Cassie and Luke really like Dad."

"Who wouldn't?" he asked, sliding off his coat and tossing it over a chair. I'd introduced the two men in my life at the beginning of the month, and they'd hit it off immediately. Talk had turned to the stock market and safety nets, and I'd zoned out almost immediately. Nearly two hours later, they'd still been going.

Incidentally, Fletcher had never found much in common with Dad, and they're rare discussions had been awkward at best.

"I can't wait for you to meet them." In the kitchen, I opened a cabinet above the stove to get a vase and struggled on my tiptoes but still couldn't reach.

"Let me." Ryan stepped up beside me and retrieved the vase with no problem.

I turned and we were close enough for me to feel his breath on my cheek. "Thank you," I said, my voice coming out as a whisper.

His lips curled up in that way that made me dizzy. "Anytime."

We stayed there, inches apart, until he said, "The flowers aren't the only present I brought you."

I tugged on the front of his shirt. "I told you not to get me anything."

"And I ignored you." Setting the vase on the island, he pulled a small box from his pocket. We were barely a month into knowing each other so there was no way the man had gotten me a ring. And yet, my heart bounced around my chest as he held up the little black box. "Happy birthday, Megan." Mouth dry, I stared into his eyes for several seconds, not sure what to say. "Open it," he urged.

Letting out a shaky breath, I took the present and slowly lifted the lid. There, on a bed of cotton, was a beautiful gold necklace.

"You got me a Squirtle necklace?"

"I had to order it, and it almost didn't come in time. That's why it isn't wrapped. I just got it today."

I slid a fingertip over his shiny gold nose. "He's so cute. I can't believe you did this."

"I know how much you like him. And you said you lost a necklace you used to wear all the time, so I figured I'd get you a new one."

How did I get so lucky to find this man?

"Will you put it on me?" I said, pulling the bauble from the box. Handing it over, I spun around and pulled up my hair. A second later, the necklace fell into place, but before I could let my hair down, warm lips kissed the back of my neck. I shivered as heat crawled up my cheeks.

"Do you like it?" he asked, dropping his chin onto my shoulder as his arms slid around my waist.

Pressing my hands over his, I sighed. "I love it." I nearly added *and I love you*, but it was far too early for that. Even if I knew to my core that it was true.

"I'm glad."

"Megan, where did you go?" said Becca, stepping into the kitchen. She stopped when she spotted us, causing Jacob to run into the back of her. Spinning back around, she pushed at his chest. "Back outside. Go. Go!"

Laughing, I rolled my eyes. "Becca, it's fine." She was gone before I got the words out. "We aren't doing anything."

"We could be," Ryan whispered in my ear.

That was for later.

"These flowers need to be in water." I slid out of his arms. I filled the vase in the sink and arranged the flowers after giving them each a quick trim. "They're beautiful."

"You're beautiful." Ryan took my hand and pulled me against his chest. "Have I told you that I really like you?"

That settled it. This was the best birthday ever.

"I really like you, too."

We didn't join the others for several more minutes, and when we did, a hush fell over the group. I pretended my lips weren't swollen from kissing the man of my dreams as I settled in to celebrate my birthday with the people who meant the world to me.

To celebrate with my family.

———

THANK you so much for reading Not Playing Fair. I hope you enjoyed the story, and that you'll post a review to let other readers know how you feel. If you want to make sure you don't miss the next book in the series, which will be wedding photographer Donna's story, hop over to Amazon now and pre-order Not the Best Man!

ACKNOWLEDGMENTS

I'm having so much run writing these stories set in my old stomping grounds of Pittsburgh. My family is still there so I get to visit every now and then, and the charm never fades. If anything, the city is even cooler now than it was when I left more than twenty-five years ago. (Yes, I'm that old, and the only reason I moved south was because we had three blizzards in eighteen months. THREE!)

I need to thank my family for answering random questions at all hours of the night, and my sister for going to a Pirates baseball game with me so I could do a little research. Sadly, I got to the end of the book and realized I'd forgotten to send the characters to a ball game. Keep an eye on the rest of the series because I *will* be doing that eventually.

Special thanks goes to librarian Beth Zovko, who was nice enough to give me an impromptu tour around the West End branch during my summer visit. If you're in the area, I highly suggest visiting this library. It's small but the history seeps out of every corner.

Thank you, as always, to my writing buddies who

help me brainstorm and regularly talk me off of various cliffs. Maureen Betita and Kim Law, thank you! And to my editor Kimberly Dawn ,who has saved me from looking bad so many times. I couldn't do this without her.

Last but never least, the readers. You all keep me going and I can't possibly convey how much I appreciate you. I am beyond blessed to get to write these books for a living, and it's thanks to you that this dream has come true.

Shooting Stars Series

Rising Star

Falling Star

Wishing On A Star

Among The Stars

Stand-Alones

Ask Me To Stay

Wrecked

Awakening Anna

ABOUT THE AUTHOR

Terri Osburn writes contemporary romance with heart, hope, and lots of humor. After landing on the bestseller lists with her Anchor Island Series, she moved on to the Ardent Springs series, which earned her a Book Buyers Best award in 2016. Terri's work has been translated into five languages, and sold more than 1.5 million copies worldwide. She resides in Pittsburgh, PA with four frisky felines and two high-maintenance terrier mixes.